THE GUNSMITH

443

Beauty and the Gun

Books by J.R. Roberts
(Robert J. Randisi)

The Gunsmith series

Lady Gunsmith series

Angel Eyes series

Tracker series

Mountain Jack Pike series

COMING SOON!

The Gunsmith
444 – Deadly Trouble

For more information visit:
www.SpeakingVolumes.us

THE GUNSMITH

443

Beauty and the Gun

J.R. Roberts

SPEAKING VOLUMES, LLC
NAPLES, FLORIDA
2019

Beauty and the Gun

ISBN 978-1-62815-968-4

Chapter One

Redwind, Texas

Clint Adams had never been to Redwind, Texas before.

He had ridden through the panhandle many times, one time coming within two miles of the town, but had never stopped there.

This time, however, he was riding across the flatlands of the panhandle with Redwind as his actual destination...

***

Days before he had been sitting in Rick's Place in Labyrinth, Texas for the third day in a row since arriving there for a break. It seemed he was doing this more often, of late. Labyrinth was the only town where he felt remotely at home. Did this mean that he was starting to look for a place to settle down? Was he tired of riding the trail, finding trouble, if not looking for it?

"What are you thinkin'?" Rick asked, as he walked by. "You look like you're in pain."

"Maybe I am." Clint picked up his beer and finished it.

"Hayley!" Rick called. "Bring Clint another one."

"Yes, Boss."

Hayley, a girl Rick had hired since the last time Clint was in Labyrinth, hurried over with a full mug and set it down in front of him.

"Bring me a coffee, will you?" Rick asked her.

"Yes, Boss."

He sat across from Clint.

"We've done this before," Clint said.

"We do it every time you come home," Rick said.

"Home?"

"Well," Rick said, "home for me. Not for you, of course." Hayley brought his coffee and left. "You don't have a home. I mean, you don't want a home . . . do you?"

Clint thought about the question, then said, "No, I don't. At one time I probably thought I did, but not anymore. I've spent too many years in the saddle."

"The saddle," Rick repeated.

"Wait a minute," Clint said. "That's it."

"What's it?"

"The saddle," Clint said, as if suddenly struck by a brilliant thought. "The saddle's my home."

"You know," Rick said, "that makes sense. It's where you're the most comfortable, isn't it?"

"Yeah," Clint said, "yeah, it is."

"Of course," Rick said, "it's where trouble always finds you."

"Maybe," Clint said, "but I've done plenty of riding with no trouble, at all."

"Maybe so," Rick said, "but how often have you received a telegram that didn't bring you trouble?"

"Why would you ask that?"

Rick pointed to the batwing doors, where the telegraph key operator had just entered.

"Could be for you," Clint said.

"Telegram for Mr. Adams," the clerk said.

"Thank you," Clint said, accepting it.

"A beer before you go, Lon?" Rick asked.

"No thanks," the young clerk said, "I gotta get back."

"Have a good day," Rick said.

"You, too."

Lon left as Clint unfolded the telegram.

"Trouble?" Rick asked.

It wasn't trouble. It was from Redwind, Texas with an odd request.

"Have you heard of Redwind before?" Rick asked.

"It's in the panhandle," Clint said. "I've passed close by it once or twice."

"And what do they want?"

"They want me to be a judge."

"A court judge?" Rick asked. "Don't you have to know the law for that?"

"I know the law, Rick," Clint said, "but no, not that kind of judge. The judge of a contest."

"What kind of contest?" Rick asked. "Shooting?"

"No."

Rick thought.

"Pie?"

"That would be good," Clint said, "but no."

"Then what?" Before Clint could answer, Rick brightened and asked, "Beer?"

"Girls!" Clint said.

"What?"

"I don't have all the details," Clint said, "but they want me to come and judge girls."

"Doing what?" Rick asked.

"Being girls, I think," Clint said. "Saloon girls. Being pretty. Serving drinks."

"Well, you know about that," Rick said, "but not as much as I do. I wonder why they didn't ask me?"

"If they did," Clint asked, "would you go?"

"No."

"Well, there you are," Clint said. "So they invited me."

"Are you gonna go?" Rick asked.

"Somebody's asking me to come and look at pretty girls, and not wanting me to shoot anybody or figure out who killed somebody, or track somebody down? Why not?"

***

So here he was, riding to the town of Redwind, Texas. He had sent them a telegram saying that he would ride in, but wouldn't make a decision about doing the judging until he got there.

As he approached Redwind, he could see from a distance that the town had several two-story structures. Getting closer he also saw that it was spread out pretty far. It was obviously a growing town, and maybe this contest was a way for them to keep on growing. Having the Gunsmith judge their contest would surely get them some notice.

When Clint rode into town it was midday and things were busy. The street seemed crowded and the boardwalk was full of people hurrying back and forth. He wondered how many of these people were actually in town for the contest?

Chapter Two

A second telegram had told Clint there would be a room waiting for him in the Wayfarer Hotel. He reined in Eclipse in front and dismounted. Taking his saddlebags and rifle into the lobby with him, he had to make a quick move to avoid being bumped by a middle-aged man and woman who were hurrying out. Inside, the lobby was busy.

There was a man at the front desk, who turned angrily and stormed away, much the way the middle-aged couple had.

"I'm sorry, sir," the clerk said to him when he stepped up to the desk, "we're full up."

"Is that what you told the people before me?" Clint asked. "That man, and the couple?"

"Yes, and they didn't take it real well," the man said. "I hope you'll take it better."

"I will," Clint said, "because I know I have a room waiting. Or, I'm supposed to."

"What?"

"Clint Adams?"

The clerk, in his late 20s, suddenly lifted his eyebrows and his mouth opened.

"You're the Gunsmith?" he asked, when he had re-covered.

"I am."

"Well, yessir!" the clerk said. "You do have a room. It's on the top floor, right at the front, so you can see the street from th—"

"That won't do," Clint said. "I'll need a room away from the front."

"Uh, but that's the best room in the hotel," the clerk said. "I was told—"

"I know what you were told," Clint said. "I'll just take a smaller room."

"B-but, we don't have any others—"

"Do you have a young couple in any of your rooms?" Clint asked.

"Uh, well, we do," the clerk said. "How did you know?"

"Just a lucky guess," Clint said. "Why don't you tell them that they can have the big room in front, and put me in their room. Can you do that?"

"Uh, well, I guess they wouldn't mind."

"Good. Here." He handed the clerk his saddlebags but kept his rifle. "Put those in my room while I take care of my horse. That should give you time to make the switch."

"Uh, well, yessir, all right—"

"And don't worry," Clint said. "I'll take full responsibility for the change."

"Yessir," the clerk said, "thank you sir."

"Where do I take my horse?" Clint asked. "I understand that's been arranged, as well?"

The clerk gave him directions.

***

Clint took Eclipse down to a seemingly crowded livery stable, but when he told the man who he was the hostler said, "Oh sure, I've got a stall for your horse. It's in the back where he won't be crowded."

"And are all these people here for this contest?" Clint asked.

"Oh yeah," the middle-aged man said, "this contest is gonna be big for our town."

"Have they done this before?" Clint asked. "Had a contest like this?"

"Not here."

"What do you mean?"

"There's a bigger contest in Fort Worth," the hostler said. "Whoever wins this one goes there to compete."

"And how do you know this?" Clint asked.

"Easy," the man said. "My daughter's in the contest. Beautiful girl."

"I see."

"You're gonna be one of the judges, right?"

"That's not definite, yet," Clint said.

"Well, if ya are, I'll introduce you to my Betty," the man said.

"I'll look forward to it," Clint said.

Already having second thoughts, he left the livery and headed back to the hotel.

Chapter Three

When Clint got back to the hotel the desk clerk happily handed him the key to his new room.

"Top of the stairs, Mr. Adams," he said. "Not anywhere near the front."

"Thank you," Clint said, "Do you know where I can find Randall Flatt?"

"Mr. Flatt would be at City Hall."

"He's not the mayor, is he?" Clint asked.

"No, sir, but he's runnin' the contest from there," the clerk said. "It's the only place big enough."

"Okay," Clint said, "so I guess I'll go on over there to talk to him."

"Oh, wait!" the clerk said, as Clint started toward the stairs. "I forgot to give you this message."

Clint reached back and accepted the envelope from the man.

"Thanks."

"Yessir!"

He didn't open the envelope until he was upstairs in his room.

The message was from Randall Flatt, asking Clint to meet him at the Redwind Steakhouse for supper at 8 p.m.

It was midday and he was hungry now. He had plenty of time to get something to eat before meeting Flatt for supper.

He left his rifle in the room with his saddlebags and went back downstairs.

"Where's a good place to get something to eat?" he asked the clerk.

"But . . . Mr. Flatt wants you to have supper with him," the young man said.

"That's later," Clint said. "I'm hungry now."

"Well, just down the street is a café that does great lunch," the clerk said. "Out the door and to the right."

"Okay, thanks."

Clint left the hotel lobby, which was still filled with disappointed people who couldn't get rooms. Outside he got jostled a few times as he walked down the street, eyes alert for the café the clerk had told him about. It was a lucky thing he had been looking or he would have missed the tiny place. But as he walked in, large aromas came into his nostrils, and his stomach began to growl.

There were five tables in the small room, and they were all taken. But at that moment, a man and woman stood up and walked out, so Clint was able to claim the table.

"Let me clean that for you, sir," a pretty waitress said, running over.

"Thank you."

She cleared away the dishes and used a rag to wipe off the top of the table. It wasn't against a wall, but he was able to sit so he could see the front door and have nobody behind him.

The waitress came running back and asked. "What can I get you, sir?"

"If my nose isn't fooling me, I think I smell beef stew," Clint said.

"No, sir, your nose isn't lying to you," she said. "We have very good beef stew."

"Then I'll have a bowl, with some bread."

The girl beamed at him, her face lighting up, and she said, "Comin' up, sir. How about somethin' to drink?"

"Coffee," Clint said, "a pot of strong coffee."

"Right away."

The girl scurried away to the kitchen and returned quickly with a pot and a mug.

"That was fast," Clint observed. "I hope it's strong."

"It's the only way we make it," she assured him, pouring him a cup.

She went back to the kitchen and Clint tried the coffee. It was very good, as strong as he wanted it.

When she brought the beef stew and bread, he dug in figuring he had already found his favorite place to eat in Redwind.

When he paid his bill the girl said, "You come back, now."

"If all the food is as good as this, I will," he promised.

"Oh, it is!" she said, enthusiastically.

"Then I'll see you soon."

He left the café and walked back to his hotel. He had nothing to do until his meeting with Randall Flatt, and he didn't want to spend the time on the crowded streets. He thought he might as well go to his room, read, and maybe catch a short nap.

***

Refreshed from what had turned into a long nap, Clint came down to the lobby at 7:30. There was a new clerk at the desk, an older man, and the lobby itself was almost deserted. Apparently, all the people complaining about not being able to get a room had either found something, or simply left.

"Excuse me," he said to the clerk.

"Yes, sir?" The man looked up at him. "It's Mr. Adams, isn't it?"

"That's right."

"What can I do for you, sir?"

"You can point me toward the Redwind Steakhouse."

"I can do that," the clerk said, and did.

Chapter Four

When Clint reached the Steakhouse he looked around, saw that all the tables were occupied. He took a few guesses about which man would be Randall Flat, then told a waiter he was there to meet him.

"Oh yes, sir," the waiter said. "This way."

He had spotted two men, each seated alone, wearing expensive looking suits, and thought one of them might be Flatt. He was wrong.

The waiter took him to a table where a man was seated, who looked more like a store clerk than a . . . it occurred to Clint that all he knew about Randall Flatt was that he sent him the telegrams and was in charge of the contest. He didn't know what the man did for a living.

"Clint Adams?"

"That's right," Clint said, after the waiter had led him to a table. "Mr. Flatt?"

"Randall." Flatt stood up and extended his hand. It was the hand of a laborer. He was in his 40s and had obviously worked hard all his life.

"Clint."

"Have a seat, Clint," Flatt said.

He sat across from the man, who reseated himself.

"When did you get in?" Flatt asked.

"This afternoon."

"Then you've seen how the town is reacting to this contest."

"The hotels are full, and so are the streets," Clint said.

"As well as the restaurants and saloon," Flatt said. "This is a success."

"Then you're to be congratulated," Clint said.

Flatt hesitated a moment, then said, "I'm not what you expected, am I?"

"Frankly, no," Clint said. "I thought a banker, a politician . . ."

". . . or maybe a saloon owner," Flatt finished. "I'm none of those things. I own and run the mercantile."

"So you're a businessman?"

"I am," Flatt said, "and I'm on the town council. But I'm not a politician, and definitely not a banker. I'm just one of the citizens trying to do something for Redwind."

"And getting it done, it seems," Clint said.

"You can help me with that," Flatt said, "if you'll agree to be a judge."

"How many judges will there be?" Clint asked.

"Three."

"Who are the others?"

"I'll tell you that after you agree to be number three," Flatt said. "And I hope you don't mind, but I ordered supper."

The waiter came with two steaming plates bearing huge steaks and a large amount of vegetables.

"I don't mind at all," Clint said.

"So let's eat and talk," Flatt said, "and when we're done, you can tell me your decision. And no matter what it is, your hotel room is free for as long as you want it."

"That's very generous of you."

"And, of course," Flatt said, "this supper is on the town."

"Then let's eat."

***

Clint was shocked at how good the meal was, right down to the apple pie Flatt had also ordered.

"This town has pretty good food," Clint observed.

"We do," Flatt said. "Did you eat somewhere else?"

"Oh," Clint said. "just a small snack when I arrived."

"Where?"

"A small cafe near my hotel."

"Well, you're right," Flatt said, "we have good food, good people, and the prettiest girls."

"Isn't that what the contest is supposed to decide?" Clint asked.

"No," Flatt said. "We know we have pretty girls—no, beautiful girls. But the point is to find the prettiest and send her to Fort Worth."

"And how big is that contest?" Clint asked.

"Big," Flatt said. "There'll be women from towns all over Texas competing. We have to send the best one we have." Flatt was warming to his subject. "That's why I want you, Clint. You have a reputation with women."

"Well . . ."

"Oh, I know, you have more of a reputation with a gun, but the point is, you know beautiful women. And we need to pick out our best. We need you."

"And the other two?"

"We have two more judges, just to make it fair," Flatt said. "But your word is gonna carry the most weight."

"I see."

"If you agree," Flatt said. "I can introduce you to the other judges right away."

Clint hesitate, then figured, why not?

"We'd better get started, then."

Chapter Five

The first judge was the mayor.

"I couldn't say no," Flatt said, as he and Clint left the steakhouse. "He's a true politician and saw this as a vote gathering event."

"Will he be honest?" Clint asked.

"I said he's a politician, didn't I?" Flatt asked.

"So he's got chips in the game."

"Let's just say he's not related to any of the girls," Flatt said, "but I'm sure he's got a favorite."

"But he's still a judge."

"I'm just gonna have to put more value on what you and the other judge say."

"Okay," Clint said, "and who's that?"

"You two will meet after I take you to the mayor's house," Flatt said. "He's waitin' for us."

So he led the way to another part of town where a large house stood out in amongst the smaller ones that surrounded it.

"It's new," Flatt said. "The mayor had it built after he won the election."

"And when was that?"

"Two years ago."

"What's his name?"

"Mayor Hubert Hunter," Flatt said. "When he was running, he put out posters and fliers that said 'Vote for Hubie.'"

They went up to the front door and Flatt knocked. It was opened by a tall, thin man with white hair who Clint took as a servant, due to the white gloves he was wearing.

"Randall!" the man said. "Come in, come in!"

As they entered Flatt said, "Mr. Mayor, meet Clint Adams. Clint, Mayor Hunter."

Surprised, Clint shook the politician's hand.

"Mr. Mayor," he said, not bothering to say it was a pleasure to meet him, because it was never a pleasure to meet a politician.

"Thank you for coming to Redwind, Mr. Adams," the mayor said. "And for agreeing to judge our contest." The mayor frowned. "You have agreed, haven't you?"

"I have."

"Both of you come with me," he said, and led the way through the house to a room lined with full book shelves.

"Drink?" the mayor asked. "I have the best cognac, the best wine, the best bourbon—"

"None for me, thanks," Clint said.

"Me, neither," Flatt said.

The mayor shrugged and poured himself a snifter of cognac. Clint wanted to ask about the white gloves, but he decided to wait.

"Sit gentlemen," the mayor said, sitting behind a desk, "let's talk."

"It sounds to me like this contest is very important to your town, Mayor," Clint said, seating himself.

"Indeed," Mayor Hunter said. "Randall has come up with a marvelous concept."

"Not mine," Flatt said. "We're just trying to follow the Fort Worth example."

"And he's modest," Hunter said, "that's why I put him in charge of the event."

"Well, he seems to know what he's doing so far," Clint said, "but I only arrived this afternoon."

"What do you think of our little town?"

"It's busy."

"Ha! That's because of the contest." The mayor looked at Flatt. "Has he met the other judge yet?"

"No," Flatt said, "I'm gonna do that when we leave here."

"Well, it's getting late, so you better do that," the mayor said. "I'll walk you to the door."

He saw them out the front door, said good-night, and once again said to Clint, "Thank you for coming."

As he closed the door, Clint and Flatt walked back to the street.

"What's going on with the white gloves?" Clint asked.

"He has this fear of dirt," Flatt said. "Always wears a pair of gloves. When he's home they're white, when he's out and about, they're grey or black."

"Well," Clint said, "if he's afraid of dirt, he's in the wrong business."

Randall Flatt laughed.

***

Flatt took him to another part of town, and a smaller house.

"For a second judge I chose another business owner in town," he said. "So we have two locals, and you, someone who has no chips in the game, as you said."

Clint looked the one-story house over.

"What business do they own?" he asked.

"The dress shop," Flatt said, and knocked on the door.

Since the business was a dress shop, Clint was not as surprised as he might have been when a woman opened the door.

Chapter Six

"Randall," the woman said. "How nice."

"Rita," he said, "this is Clint Adams, our third judge."

"So Mr. Adams has agreed to take part?"

"He has."

"You'd better come in, then."

Flatt entered, with Clint close behind. As he passed the woman, he caught her scent, which seemed to have been freshly applied. It smelled like roses.

She closed the door and then turned to face them.

"Clint, this is Miss Rita Mason," Flatt said. "She owns the dress store on Main Street. Rita, this is Clint Adams. He's—"

"I know who Mr. Adams is," she said, extending her hand. She smiled at Clint. "It's a pleasure to meet you."

"The pleasure's mine, Mrs. Mason."

"Oh, Rita, please," she said. "Since we're both judges, you should call me Rita."

"And I'm Clint."

"Please, gentlemen, come in," Rita said. "Randall, since you told me you'd be dropping by with Mr. Adams, I made coffee."

"That sounds good," Clint said.

"Yes, it does," Flatt agreed.

"Then follow me, please," she said. "We'll go right to the dining room."

She walked ahead of them, and Clint watched the sway of her hips. She appeared to be in her late thirties, with honey-colored hair piled atop her head. She was wearing a blue dress he assumed came from her store. It fit her perfectly, covering her from neck to ankles, but doing nothing to hide the curves of her body, which seemed plentiful.

The "dining room" was not a room on its own, but part of the living room. There was a round wooden table with four chairs around it on one side, and a sofa and matching chair on the other. It was good furniture, though not expensive.

"Please, sit," she said. "I'll get the coffee."

As they seated themselves at the table she went to the kitchen and returned carrying a tray with a pot of coffee and cups.

She poured them each a cup, offered cream and sugar—which both men refused—then sat with them and doctored her own coffee with a lot of sugar.

"So," she said to Clint, "what do you think?"

"Of the town?" he asked. "Or the contest?"

"Both," she said, "as well as our mayor. I assume you went to his house first."

"We did," Flatt said.

"The mayor strikes me as a politician, pure and simple," Clint said.

"Oh, he is," she said. "And why do I get the feeling you don't like politicians?"

"Because I don't," he said. "As for the town, it's busy, and seems to be growing. The contest looks to be bringing people in, which will benefit everybody."

"That's for sure."

"And probably you most, of all," he went on.

"Me? Why me?" she asked.

"You own a dress shop," Clint said. "I assume all the girls who enter the contest are going to need dresses."

"You are so right," she said. "I'm doing very well, but that's got nothing to do with why I agreed to be a judge."

Clint held up his hand.

"I'm here to judge the girls, not you," he said. "Your reasons are your own."

"But I'm curious," she said, "so can I ask you for your reasons?"

"Simple. This is unlike anything I've ever done," he said. "And to be very truthful, since I've ridden all this way, I might as well stay and do it."

"That's a good enough reason for me," Flatt said. "We needed an outsider."

"Yes, we did," Rita said.

"So when does this start?" Clint asked.

24

"We have a party tomorrow night to introduce all the girls," Flatt said. "Then the judging will begin the next morning."

"I have to say," Rita said, "that my judging will start at the party. I want to see how these girls interact with each other, and everyone else."

"Nothing wrong with that," Flatt said.

Clint didn't comment. He didn't know if he would do that as well or save his judging eye for the actual start of the competition.

"I know that however you two judge the contest, you'll do it fairly," Flatt said.

"You can't say that about the mayor, huh?" Clint asked.

"The mayor is going to do whatever is best for the mayor," Rita said.

"It's up to you two to do whatever's best for the girls, for the contest, and for the town," Flatt said.

"I think we can do that," Rita said, "don't you, Clint?"

"I know we can."

Chapter Seven

Clint and Flatt left Rita's house with Clint looking forward to judging with her and seeing her again.

"She's a lovely woman," Clint said.

"I thought you'd notice that," Flatt said.

"Is there something I should know?" Clint asked. "Something between you two?"

"Oh, no, nothing like that," Flatt said. "I have a wife. You'll meet her at the party tomorrow night. Or if you happen to come to my store tomorrow."

"Since nothing happens until tomorrow night, I might take a walk around town tomorrow," Clint said, "so I'll try to stop in."

"I'll tell her," Flatt said. "If I let you surprise her, I'll never hear the end of it."

Flatt was walking Clint back to his hotel, but before they got there Clint asked, "I think I'll have a beer before I go back to my room. You want to join me?"

"Why not?"

"Good," Clint said, "then you can choose the saloon."

"I know just the one!"

***

Randall Flatt took Clint to the Gun Barrel Saloon. As soon as they entered, Clint knew why. It was large, crowded, and had beautiful saloon girls working the floor ferociously.

"These are our girls," Flatt said.

"All of them?"

"Oh no," the man said, "but this is a good sampling."

"They're beautiful."

"Come on," Flatt said, "I'll get you that beer."

They went to the bar where Flatt ordered two beers and introduced Clint to the bartender.

"Mark Gardner."

They shook hands.

"You're the Gunsmith," Gardner said, "and our third judge."

"Right both times."

"Welcome!"

"Thanks."

Flatt and Clint picked up their beers and turned to look at the crowd.

"See how they make the customers happy?" Flatt asked.

"That's their job, Randall," Clint said. "They're saloon girls."

"Exactly!"

"What's that mean?"

"I wanted you to see them in action."

"Tell me," Clint said, "what am I going to be judging? I mean, what will they be doing?"

"We have a few categories," Flatt said, "but I probably should wait until I can tell you, Rita and the mayor at the same time."

"That makes sense. I have another question," Clint said. "Is it only saloon girls who are entered?"

"Yes, every girl has to have a job in one of the saloons. Why?"

"I already heard from the man at the livery that he has a relative in the contest."

"That would be Lester," Flatt said. "What did he say?"

"That his daughter was competing."

Flatt frowned.

"I know he has a daughter, but I didn't know she worked in a saloon," Flatt said. "I'll have to look into this."

A girl came over to them and said, "'evenin', Mr. Flatt."

"Amy," Flatt said.

She was a young, pretty blonde with a dazzling smile.

"Is there anythin' I can do for you, Mr. Flatt?" she asked. "And who's your friend?"

"Amy," Flatt said. "You shouldn't be talking to me before the contest. And never mind who my friend is. You go back to work and tell the other girls not to come up to us. Understand?"

Amy pouted.

"I was jus' tryin' to be nice," she said.

"Oh sure," Flatt said, "I get it. Nice. Thanks very much, Amy."

She moved away from them, and Clint saw her join three of the other girls on the other side of the room.

"They must've heard you're a judge," Flatt said. "Look, be real careful tonight."

"About what?" Clint asked. "Usually, I'm careful not to get shot in the back."

"Well," Flatt said, "I don't think that's gonna happen, but I wouldn't put it past these girls to come to your room and try to influence you."

"Ah, I get it," Clint said. "I tell you what, I won't open my door if somebody knocks."

"I need you to promise that," Flatt said. "Don't open it, and don't have anything to do with any of the saloon girls in town—until the contest is over."

Clint raised his right hand and said, "I promise. No girls, and I won't open my door."

"Unless it's me," Flatt said.

"Well, in that case," Clint said, "why don't we work out a secret knock?"

Clint was kidding, but Randall Flatt said, "That's a great idea."

Chapter Eight

Both of them decided that Clint shouldn't be left alone at the Gun Barrel saloon, so after they finished their beers, Flatt walked him back to his hotel.

"Remember the knock," Flatt said, in the lobby.

"I'll remember."

"And I'm gonna instruct the desk clerks not to tell anyone what room you're in."

"Whatever you say, Randall," Clint said. "You're in charge."

Clint went up to his room, thinking he probably wouldn't have minded if one or more of the girls came to his room that night to try to influence him.

But once inside his room he was determined to stick to his promise to Randall Flatt.

No girls.

And no opening his door.

He removed his boots, unbuttoned his shirt, hung his gunbelt on the bedpost, and then sat on the bed with a book. He was currently reading *The Moonstone* by Wilkie Collins. He found where he had left off, read a couple more chapters, and then put it down and went to sleep.

No one knocked on his door.

***

In the morning Clint walked down the street to the same little café to have breakfast.

"Good morning," the same waitress greeted.

"'morning."

He looked around. Unlike yesterday, the place was empty.

"You can have whichever table you want today," she told him.

"That one, against the wall."

"Have a seat. I'll bring your coffee."

"And steak-and-eggs," Clint said.

"Biscuits?"

"Yes, please."

"Comin' up," she promised.

He sat and relaxed. The girl brought the coffee first followed by a basket of warm biscuits and, finally, the steak-and-eggs platter.

"Anything else?" she asked.

"No, this looks great."

"Well, my name's Penelope," she said. "If you need anythin' else, just call."

"I will. Thanks."

While he was eating, several other people came in and sat. At one table was a middle-aged couple, and at the other an older man, by himself. Penelope took their orders and served them as quickly as she had served Clint. She was apparently very efficient. Clint thought she would be a good contestant for a Best Waitress contest.

Breakfast was just as good as the beef stew had been the day before.

"More coffee?" Penelope asked, coming over to his table with a pot.

"Please." She had given him a cup earlier, but not left the pot. Now she refilled his cup.

"Can I ask you a question?" she asked.

"Sure."

She sat across from him.

"Are you one of the judges for the saloon girl contest?"

"Who told you that?"

She shrugged. "I heard it."

"Well, I am," he said. "Don't tell me you also work in one of the saloons."

"Oh, no," she said. "Not me. I'm not pretty enough for that."

"And who told you that?" Clint asked. "You're very pretty."

"No, no," she said, "not to be a saloon girl. But my sister, she's very pretty."

"And she's a saloon girl?"

"Yes," Penelope said. "She works in the Gun Barrel."

Clint studied Penelope for a moment, her clear skin and blonde hair, and then asked, "Is her name Amy?"

Penelope looked surprised.

"How did you know that?"

"I met her last night," Clint said, "and she reminds me of you. So when you mentioned your sister, I took a guess."

"Then you saw how pretty she is."

"Is she younger?"

Penelope nodded.

"She's two years younger. She's twenty-two, and I'm twenty-four."

"Do you think she has a chance to win?" Clint asked.

"Oh, I know she does," Penelope said. "But I'm worried what will happen to her if she goes to Fort Worth. I mean . . . that's not a little town."

"No," Clint agreed, "it's not."

"I guess the question is," Penelope said, "do you think she has a chance to win?"

"I don't know, Penelope," he said. "I haven't seen all the girls, yet."

"Of course." She stood up. "It was a silly question. And you can call me Penny, from now on."

"And you can call me Clint."

"Will I see you later, Clint?"

He stood up.

"You just might."

Chapter Nine

As he had told Flatt he would, Clint took a walk around town. He was intending to stop in at Flatt's mercantile, but before coming to it, he saw Rita Mason's dress shop. He assumed it was hers, because he couldn't imagine there being two in town.

The store was called MISS RITA'S DRESS SHOP, which made more sense than many other businesses he had seen over the years.

He crossed the street to take a look through the windows. There were dresses draped on dummies. Further inside he could see some intimate items, which were not on display in the window.

He decided to go in.

A bell rang above the door as he entered, and three women turned to look at him. One of them was Rita Mason. She was standing with a woman in her 50s, and another who looked to possibly be 20.

"I'll be with you in a minute, sir," Rita said, with an amused smile on her face.

"Take your time," he said. "I'll browse."

The older woman was apparently buying some dresses for her daughter, who kept glancing over at Clint, and then quickly looking away. Although she was a pretty girl, when she got older she was probably going to be a little thick in the waist and hips, like her mother. It was too bad.

Rita finished with the women, assured the mother that the dresses would be ready very soon. The look the mother gave him on the way out was disapproving. That was when he realized he was standing in front of a display of corsets. The daughter blushed as she walked past him.

"Regular customers?" Clint asked Rita.

"I'm afraid so."

"Why afraid?"

"Mrs. Kennelly is a hard woman to satisfy."

"Doesn't the daughter get a say about her dresses?" Clint asked.

"You'd think so, but no. Billie hasn't yet decided to stand up to her mother." She turned and walked back around to the other side of her counter. "What brings you here, this morning? An interest in intimate apparel?"

Clint looked again at the corset he was standing in front of, then moved away from it.

"No, not at all," he said. "I was just taking a walk around town, since we judges won't have anything to do until this evening."

"Well, this judge does," she corrected him. "I'll be open until five, and the party starts at seven."

She stared at him expectantly, and he thought he knew what she had on her mind.

"I have an idea," he said. "Why don't we have supper together before the party? Talk a little bit about our strategies for judging the contest."

"Why, that sounds like a lovely idea, Mr. Adams," she said.

"And if we're going to share a meal," he said, "you'll have to call me Clint."

"I think I can do that," she said, "if you'll call me Rita."

"You've got a deal," he said. "Should I meet you at your house?"

"Why don't you come here and collect me just after five," she suggested. "Then we can go right to supper."

"Sounds good," he said. "I'll see you a little after five."

As he was leaving, another customer entered, a woman in her thirties with a pleasant expression on her face. Clint tipped his hat to her.

***

Several streets from Miss Rita's Dress Shop Clint found the Mercantile Store. There were all sorts of tools on display outside—pick axes, shovels, axe handles—

along with barrels and crates. A man and a woman came out, the woman carrying something wrapped in brown paper, while the man kept a possessive hand on her arm. And just ahead of Clint a big, brawny man stormed into the store, and seemed to have something on his mind. Clint plucked an axe handle from the barrel they were displayed in and followed.

Inside there were other customers milling about. A woman was behind the counter wearing a white apron and waiting on an older male customer. Clint didn't see Randall Flatt anywhere.

The brawny man bumped a couple of men aside and charged the counter, also elbowing the customer.

"What the hell are you tryin' ta pull?" he demanded of the woman.

"Sam, I have other customers ahead of you." She was a handsome woman in her 40s, and seemed very calm in the face of the much larger Sam.

"But I ain't a customer, am I?" Sam demanded. "At least, that's what you told my boy when I sent him here with a list."

"Sam," she said, "you owe us quite a bit of money."

"And I'm good fer it!" he snapped. "You know that!"

"Sam, all we're asking is a portion of what you owe, and we'll carry you for the rest. We just can't—"

"Yer embarrasin' me, is what yer doin'," he said. "In front of my boy, my wife, my men, and these people here."

"I think you're embarrassing yourself right now, Sam."

"You think 'cause yer a woman I won't turn this counter over on ya?" he demanded. "Where's yer husband hidin'?"

"Randall's in the back, doing some inventory," she said. "You'll have to deal with me, Sam, and if you want to overturn my counter, go ahead. We'll add the damage to your bill."

The woman seemed very confident that she was in command, but when the man's right hand shot out and grabbed her by the white apron, the look of confidence faded.

"How about I bust you up, instead?" he asked.

"N-now, Sam—"

"Hey, Sam, take it easy—" the customer she had been waiting on said, but Sam swung his left arm and back-handed the man right across the face, knocking him off his feet.

The other customers in the store quickly departed, leaving Sam with the woman still in his grasp, the older customer on the floor bleeding from his lip, and Clint.

"Who's gonna save ya now?" Sam sneered.

"I am," Clint said.

Chapter Ten

Sam turned to look over his shoulder at Clint, still maintaining his hold on the woman, who was trying to dislodge herself. She had both hands on his arm but wasn't making any progress.

"Stay outta this, stranger," he growled.

"Afraid I can't do that," Clint said. "That's no way to treat a woman. Now let her go."

"Ya want me ta bust you up after I finish with her?" Sam asked.

"You can try."

"And whataya gonna do, shoot me? I ain't armed."

"I won't need to shoot you, Sam," Clint said. "Now let her go."

"Make me!"

Clint brought the axe handle up as Sam turned his attention back to the woman dangling from his big hand. Stepping to his left, Clint brought the handle down on Sam's right arm, the one he was holding the woman with.

He hit him on the bicep, and when Sam yelled "Ow!" and released the woman, Clint hit him again, this time on the elbow.

"Jesus!" Sam shouted, grabbing for his arm. "What the hell—"

"I think you better leave the store, Sam," the woman said. "And don't come back. Do your shopping somewhere else from now on. You're banned."

"I dunno what that means," Sam snapped at her, "but you can bet you won't be gettin' no more of my money."

"We're not getting a lot of it right now, are we, Sam?" she asked.

Sam turned to glare at Clint.

"You made a big mistake today, Mister," he said. "The next time I see you, I'll have a gun."

"And that'll be your big mistake," Clint assured him.

Sam bolted for the door and stormed out, still holding onto his arm.

The woman breathed a sigh of relief and looked at Clint.

"Thank you so much," she said. "I really thought he was going to hit me."

"Is your husband really in the back?" Clint asked.

"No," she said, "he's over at City Hall working on that silly contest. That's why I have to thank you, Mister—"

"Adams," he said. "Clint Adams."

"Randall said you might be stopping by," she said, with a smile. "I'm glad you did. My name's Adele."

They shook hands. When they heard a moan, they both looked down and remembered the man on the floor.

"Oh, Floyd" she said, hurrying around the counter.

She and Clint helped the man up.

"Are you all right?" she asked.

"I think so," the old man said.

"Thank you so much for trying to help me," she said. "Maybe you'd better go home and take care of that lip. I'll fill your order and you can pick it up tomorrow."

"Okay," he said, and staggered out the door.

"Poor Floyd," she said, going back behind the counter. "Were you looking for Randall? Or did you need to buy something?"

"Actually, I was just walking around town, found myself out front and thought I'd come inside."

"Well," she said, smoothing her hands down over her white apron, "I'm glad you did."

She stared at him for a few long moments, and then blushed, giving him some idea of what she might have been thinking. She was a handsome woman and looked to have a good body beneath that apron. If he didn't know she was married to Randall Flatt, he might have been tempted to close and lock the front door and take her right there on the counter.

Which was what he thought she might be thinking at that moment.

Chapter Eleven

"Clint!"

They both looked at the door, saw Randall Flatt, and hoped they didn't look too guilty.

"You came to see the store," Flatt said. "I'm glad you did."

"So am I," Adele said. "He saved me from being pummeled by Sam Logan."

"Logan? What happened?"

"Nothing," she said, "but only because Mr. Adams was here."

Clint waited while Adele told her story to her husband.

"Damn!" Flatt said, when she finished. "Honey, I'm sorry I wasn't here."

"If you were," she said, "Sam probably would've smashed you. I think it was better that Mr. Adams was here. He's pretty handy with an axe handle."

Flatt looked at Clint.

"I suppose we should be grateful you didn't shoot him," he said. "You might've been in jail and not able to attend the party tonight."

"Randall!" his wife scolded.

"No, no," Flatt said, "I know it's a good thing he didn't kill a man, I'm just saying . . ."

"Go to work," she told him, pointing. "Inventory."

"Right!" He looked at Clint. "See you tonight."

Flatt hurried off into the back.

"I can't wait for this contest to be over," Adele said, "so we can get back to normal."

"You don't approve?"

"Of girls being judged on their looks?" she asked. "No, I don't."

"I was told there was more to it than that."

"Really?" she asked. "You really think that'll be true in Fort Worth? And they won't just vote for the most beautiful?"

"Well," Clint said, "I guess I won't see that, because my part will be done."

"And you'll look at more than beauty, huh?" she asked him.

"There is more to women than just their looks," he told her. "I've always believed that."

"Then you're an odd man, Mr. Adams," she said.

"Odd?"

"Different," she said, "unique? Take your pick. But you're not like all the rest, are you?"

"I hope not," he said.

***

Clint was waiting outside Rita's Dress Shop at 4 minutes past 5 when Rita Mason came out and locked the door. When she turned, she was not surprised at all to see him there.

"You're on time," she said. "That was the first test."

"And I passed?"

"So far."

"Where will we be eating?" he asked.

"I'm sure Randall has taken you to the Steakhouse."

"He has."

"Well, I have another place in mind," she said.

"Lead the way, then. I'm in your hands."

"Good," she said, with a smile, "because that was the second test."

"And I passed that one, too?"

"You did."

"I'm doing okay, so far."

"Yes, you certainly are." She linked her arm in his. "Do you mind?"

Since it was not his gun arm, he said, "I don't mind at all."

***

They walked through town arm-in-arm, drawing looks from some of the locals. This time of the evening many of the shops had closed, and foot traffic was greatly reduced. In addition, there was only an occasional horse or wagon going by on the street.

Rita nodded and exchanged greetings with a few people, mostly couples, or women walking alone. Eventually, they turned down a side street and didn't run into any more foot traffic.

"Here it is," she said, stopping in front of a building with no windows. The front door was solid wood that was flaking from age.

"How do we get in?" he asked.

"We knock."

She knocked several times on the door in no particular cadence that he could detect. It was opened a crack and an eye appeared.

"Rita," a voice said, and the door was opened wide. A smooth-skinned, middle-aged black woman put her arms out and she and Rita embraced each other warmly. It was hard to guess her age, somewhere between 50 and 60, short and a bit stocky. "Who's your friend?"

"This is Clint Adams," Rita said. "Clint, this is Loretta."

"Hello, Loretta," he said.

"Mr. Adams," Loretta said in an accent he didn't recognize, "if you're a friend of Rita's, you are welcome. Please, both of you come in."

They stepped inside and she closed the door behind them and locked it.

Chapter Twelve

The inside was dark, but Clint could see light ahead of them.

"What's in here?" he asked.

"Take a deep breath," Rita told him.

He did, and the aroma of food cooking wasn't like anything he had ever smelled before.

"That smells great."

"Follow me, please," Loretta said.

She headed for the light up ahead, so Rita and Clint fell into step behind her.

When they got to the lighted room it looked like a normal diningroom, with tables and chairs and people seated at them. The diners looked up to see who was entering, but when they saw Loretta, they went back to their food.

"It's a restaurant?" Clint asked.

"A very special restaurant," Rita said.

"And you would like a table?" Loretta asked.

"Yes, please," Rita said.

She showed them to a table that had empty tables around it. The room was less than half full.

"I will be right back," Loretta promised.

Clint looked around, at the blank walls and high ceiling.

"No menus?" he asked.

"If you'll allow," she said, "I'll order for both of us."

"What kind of food will this be?" he asked. "And what's her accent?"

"It's Jamaican," Rita said.

"Jamaican?" he asked. "That's where she's from?"

Ruth nodded. "When slavery was abolished in this country, Jamaican people were brought in by some plantation owners. That didn't last long, though, and most of them went home, but some stayed. Like Loretta's family."

"Fascinating," he said, "and it smells great in here, but what's the food like?"

"Trust me," Rita said. "I'll order, and you'll enjoy it."

He sat back in his chair and looked around. The people eating looked like simple town folk, and they were digging in and not doing much talking with each other.

"All right," he said, "I'm in your hands."

"Good," Rita said.

At that moment Loretta returned and asked, Rita, "Do you know what you want?"

"Loretta," she said, "bring us whatever's on your stove."

"Wonderful," Loretta said. "And I'll bring you some tea."

As the woman walked away Clint said, "Tea?"

"It's not real tea," she said. "Not the kind you're used to. It's Hibiscus Iced Tea. Very good. You'll see."

Loretta returned with two tall glasses of tea with ice.

"Your food will be right out," she said, setting the glasses down.

"Try it," Rita said.

She watched as he lifted the glass to his mouth, smelled it, and sipped. Then he took a bigger gulp.

"Well? She asked.

"It's delicious," he said. "Very refreshing."

"I told you!" She lifted her own glass and sipped.

He saw Loretta come from what had to be the kitchen, carrying more plates than he would have thought she could carry. They were balanced up and down her arms.

"Here we go," she said, laying them out on the table. He didn't really recognize anything, except perhaps some rice and peas.

Loretta hurried back to the kitchen and returned with two empty plates for them to put their food on, and utensils.

"Enjoy," she said, pressing her hands together in front of her. Sure that her guests were happy, she turned and left.

"Um, I think she could've explained what everything was," he said.

"I can tell you that," Rita said. "That, of course, is rice and peas. There, we have some Jamaican jerk chicken. And there's some curried goat."

"Goat?"

"Goat meat," she said. "It's really very good. And over here just various vegetables. And that smell? It comes from all the Jamaican spices she cooks with."

"Goat," he said, again.

"Haven't you ever eaten goat before?" she asked. "Or mutton?"

"I think I did once, in Mexico," he said. "Although that might've been . . . dog."

"Well," she said, heaping food onto his plate with a large silver serving spoon, "if you've eaten dog, you're going to love this."

When she finished filling his plate with goat, chicken, vegetables and rice, she did the same for herself, then sat back.

"There," she said, "now we can eat."

"What's jerk chicken?" he asked.

"Oh, it's some kind of spice," she said. "I don't know exactly what, but it's so good."

Clint wasn't sure what he should taste first, but he decided to start with the chicken. He speared some and put it in his mouth, not knowing what to expect. Certainly not the explosion of flavor he got.

"Oh my God," he said. "This is great!"

"I told you."

However, he still put off tasting the curried goat. Instead, he went for the rice and peas, and the other vegetables—yams, boiled green bananas and dumplings—and found them all very good.

Then he saw her watching him.

"What?" he asked.

"When are you going to taste the goat?"

He looked at the platter, then back at her. She regarded him with raised eyebrows.

"Oh, all right," he said, jabbing his fork into a piece and lifting it to his mouth.

"Well?" she asked.

He reached out and said, "Give me that serving spoon."

Chapter Thirteen

They spoke about the competition while they continued to eat.

"So you've already met two relatives of contestants?" Rita asked.

"Yes, you?"

She held up 4 fingers.

"Three of them are customers of mine, and one is a businessman in town."

"Any pressure?" Clint asked.

"Not really, just . . . conversation about how beautiful their sister or daughter is. And you?"

"The same."

"I wonder if there will be any pressure," she said.

"If anyone tries," Clint said, "let me know."

"What will you do?" she asked. "Shoot them?"

He stared at her.

"I'm sorry," she said, realizing she had misspoken. "I was just trying to be funny."

"It's all right."

"No," she said, "I was judging you from your reputation. I apologize."

"That's what happens when you have a reputation," he told her.

"One you don't deserve?"

"Oh, I probably deserve it," he said. "At least, part of it."

"But you're not . . . the killer everyone makes you out to be, are you?" she asked. "I can tell."

"No, I'm not," he said. "What do they have for dessert, here?"

She smiled.

"Let's ask."

***

Loretta brought them a basket of Jamaican sweet buns, to which spices were added during the making. And she brought them coffee.

"It is from the blue mountains, in Jamaica," Loretta told him. "It is very popular."

Clint could see why. It was good, and strong. The buns were both sweet and spicy, as advertised.

"That was a terrific meal," Clint told Loretta when she came back.

"You had enough to eat?" she asked.

"More than enough," he said. "How much do I owe you?"

"Don't worry about that." Loretta went to Rita, kissed her cheek and embraced her. "Come back."

"I will," Rita promised.

"And bring your handsome friend," Loretta added.

"She won't have to try to convince me," Clint said, making his own promise.

***

Outside they walked back to Main Street and Clint asked, "Can I walk you home?"

"Of course."

Along the way he asked, "Why is Loretta on such a dead street, in such a hole?"

"She and other Jamaicans aren't exactly welcome in Texas," Rita said. "Or in this country, for that matter."

"That's a shame," he said. "She should have a big restaurant in San Francisco, or Denver."

"I agree."

When they reached Rita's front door they turned and faced one another on the porch.

"Would you like to come in for a drink?" she asked.

"I would," he said, "but maybe it's not a good idea."

"Because we're both judges, you mean?"

"Yes."

"Well . . . all right," she said. "I need the time to get dressed, anyway. I'll see you later, at the party."

She went inside, and he headed for his hotel, to change.

Chapter Fourteen

The party was being held in City Hall, in what looked like a large ballroom. Clint was surprised. He had expected something a little more rustic. There was music from several musicians playing violins. People weren't exactly crowding the dance floor, but they were standing around with drinks and food in their hands. Clint didn't see anyone he thought might be a contestant.

"Clint."

He turned, saw Rita approaching wearing a lavender dress that revealed her smooth shoulders.

"Whoa," Clint said. "Are you a judge, or a contestant?"

She smiled.

"Thank you for the compliment," she said. "You look nice, too."

Clint looked down at the suit he was wearing, which probably didn't fit as well as he had hoped with the gun on his hip.

"Not exactly comfortable," he said.

"Suits aren't supposed to be," she told him. "But if it helps, you don't look uncomfortable."

"Thanks."

"There are my two judges!" Randall Flatt came rushing over to them. "And looking very fancy."

Flatt had a suit on that looked ill-fitting and uncomfortable.

"Where's our third judge?" Clint asked, looking around.

"Mr. Mayor likes to make an entrance," Flatt said. "He'll be here."

"And the girls?" Clint asked.

"They'll be here, too," Flatt said, "later. They'll make their entrance after the mayor."

"Does he know that?" Rita asked.

Flatt grinned and said, "No."

Clint looked around again.

"Where's Mrs. Flatt?" he asked.

"She's at the store, finishing up the inventory," Flatt said.

Clint remembered that Flatt was supposed to be doing inventory. It probably didn't sit well with his wife that he hadn't finished.

"Don't worry," Flatt said, reading Clint's face. "She wouldn't have wanted to come here, anyway. She doesn't approve of the contest."

"So what do we do?" Clint asked.

"Just mingle with the people," Flatt said, "and talk about the contest."

"Okay," Clint said.

"And don't stay together," Flatt said. "Split up. You'll cover more ground that way. And talk the contest up!"

***

Clint and Rita did as Randall Flatt asked and mingled with the other partygoers. Some of them were excited to meet Clint and glad he was there as a judge, others seemed afraid of him. Rita seemed to attract a lot of men, and their wives weren't happy about it. Other women, obviously customers of hers, were happy to socialize with her.

There was a table set up with food on it, just small things you could pick up and eat, not meals. There was also a bar where it looked like they were only serving beer. Clint was getting himself one when the mayor made his entrance.

He wore an expensive suit, everybody could see that from across the room. Tall and thin, he still was a commanding presence.

"Mr. Mayor," Randall Flatt said, greeting him. "You made it."

"Sorry, Randall," Hunter said, "I had some last-minute business come up."

"That's okay," Flatt said. "Now that all my judges are here, I can bring in the girls."

"Good," Mayor Hunter said. "Let's see them."

Rita moved over and stood next to Clint at the bar.

Randall Flatt stood in the center of the room, and the music stopped.

"Ladies and gentlemen," he called out. "it's time for you to meet our contestants. Here they are, the most beautiful saloon girls in the county."

A door opened and brightly attired girls began to file into the room. Their gowns and hair were every color imaginable. They were tall and short, thin and voluptuous, all with a lot of skin showing.

"Are those gowns your work?" Clint asked Rita.

"Some of them," she said.

"Nice."

"Just look at what I had to work with," she said, smiling.

"They're all beautiful," Clint said.

"This isn't going to be easy, is it?" she said.

Finally, the girls were all gathered and Clint counted an even dozen. Right in the center was Amy, the waitress Penelope's sister.

"Okay," Rita said, "here we go."

Chapter Fifteen

"Ladies and gents," Randall Flatt said again, "aren't they beautiful?"

He went on to introduce each girl by name, have them step forward when called, and told the people what saloon she worked in."

"Number eleven," Rita whispered to Clint.

"What about her? She's gorgeous?"

"She's a customer of mine," Rita said. "Never worked in a saloon in her life. Apparently, one of them hired her just for this."

"Is that legal?" he asked.

She shrugged.

"As long as they work for a saloon *now*, they're eligible," she said. "I'm sure the same is true of at least another couple of these girls."

"I wonder if Randall knows?" Clint said.

"Oh," Rita said, "he knows."

The girls then were asked to walk around the room, and make a circle, so the people could see them. As they passed Clint and Rita, they all smiled directly at him.

"Oh, you're in for it now," Rita said to him.

"What do you mean?"

"Now all the girls know you're a judge," she said. "They'll be coming for you."

"Why just me?" he asked. "Why not you? And the mayor?"

"The mayor's too old, and I'm a woman," Rita said. "You're the one they're going to concentrate on."

"I think I'll be able to cope," he said.

She touched his arm.

"Of course you will."

***

For the remainder of the evening the girls came up to him to ask him to dance. He ended up dancing with all twelve. They chattered and he smiled, but he only had a real conversation with one of them.

Amy.

"I heard you met my sister, Penny?" she said, as they danced.

"Yes, I did."

"Did she say anythin'?"

"About what?"

"About me."

"Just that you were in this contest, and that you're very pretty."

"She's jealous, you know."

"Of what?"

"I've always been the pretty one."

"Really?" Clint asked. "I think you're both very pretty."

"But I'm the one in the contest," she pointed out.

"Because you work in a saloon."

"I work in a saloon because I'm pretty enough to," Amy said. "She works as a waitress."

Clint didn't see a huge difference between the two jobs, but didn't comment.

"Thank you for the dance, Mr. Adams," Amy said, and flitted away.

Rita came over to him.

"Walk me home?"

"Of course."

"Let's go now," she said. "I think we're done here. By my count, you've danced with them all."

"And my feet hurt."

She laughed, linked her arm in his, and they walked out into the night.

***

"I'm not sure I made the right decision," Clint said, as they walked.

"You mean to stay and be a judge?"

He nodded.

"Why not?"

"No matter what we decide, there are going to be people mad at us," Clint said.

"I get up every morning knowing somebody is going to be mad at me by the time I go to bed," she told him.

"That's true."

"You just have to do what you feel is right, and people will have to live with it."

"You're a smart woman," he said, as they reached her house.

"I'll tell you how smart I am," she said. "You're going to come in with me and have a drink."

"That does sound like a smart idea."

"And then we're going to bed."

"What?"

"Do I shock you?" she asked. "I know I've got to get you to bed before all those girls start banging their fists on your hotel room door."

"Rita—"

"Don't resist," she said, tugging him toward the front door. "Those girls are all young and beautiful. I have to take you while I can."

"I'm not resisting," he said, "in the slightest."

Chapter Sixteen

After everyone had gone, Randall Flatt locked the door to City Hall, turned and saw Mayor Hunter coming out of the ballroom.

"So what do you think?" Hunter asked. "How did it go?"

"It went great!" Flatt said, enthusiastically.

"Did you see the girls dancing with your Gunsmith?" Hunter said.

"Yes, I told them all to make sure they did," Flatt said.

"Come to my office with me," the mayor said, and started up the main stairs.

In his office he sat behind his desk, and Flatt took the chair across from him.

"Do you think you're going to be able to get Adams to cooperate?"

"I think so," Flatt said. "But I'll have to play it carefully."

"I understand," Hunter said. "You are the one in charge, aren't you?"

"Yes," Flatt said, "I am."

"I suppose you'd better go home now," Mayor Hunter said. "Your wife will be wondering where you are."

"And you?"

Hunter smiled grimly.

"No wife to wonder about me," he said, "so I'll sit here for a while."

Flatt stood up.

"Good-night, then," he said. "I'll see you tomorrow as we start the competition."

"Good-night."

***

When they got inside, they were both too eager to pause for a drink. Rita took him right to her bedroom.

Hurriedly, they came together in the center of the room in a kiss that went on for some time. Then she started to undo the buttons on his shirt, while he worked on hers. But when she went for the buckle on his gunbelt, he stopped her.

"I'll do it," he said. The headboard of the bed was too smooth to hang the holster on, so he looked for a place within easy reach.

"Is there a problem?"

"I just have to be arm's length from my gun at all times," he said.

"Even in bed?"

He looked at her.

"At all times."

"Okay, wait."

She left the room, came back quickly carrying a wooden chair. She set it down near the bed, and he hung the gunbelt on the back of it.

"Is that all right?" she asked.

"That's fine."

They went back to working on each other's clothes and this time, when she went for his belt buckle, he didn't bother to interfere.

***

When Randall Flatt entered his house, he found his wife sitting on the sofa, holding a glass with a brown liquid in it. From past experience he assumed it was bourbon.

"How did your little party go?" she asked.

"It went fine," he said.

"Did the people like all the girls?"

"They did," he said. "And all the girls danced with Clint Adams."

"Hmm, trying to win him over already, are they?" she asked.

"Obviously."

"He better double lock the door of his hotel room," she said.

He sat in a chair opposite her.

"How was inventory?" he asked.

"You mean the job you were supposed to finish?" she asked, tapping her finger on the side of her glass.

"I told you I had to—"

"I know, I know," she said, "you promised the mayor you'd take care of this little contest."

"It's not little," he said, "and it's a competition, not a contest."

"Oh, whatever you want to call it," she said, dismissively. She stood and drained her drink. "I'm going to bed. Are you coming?"

"Yes," Flatt said, "in a little while."

"Try not to wake me when you do."

She walked to the kitchen to leave her glass, then went to the bedroom, leaving him alone.

He sat back in his chair and thought about the activities of the evening. The girls had all done themselves proud, and the townspeople in attendance had reacted well. Now all he had to do was get things started the next day, with contestants and judges all in place.

Chapter Seventeen

Rita Mason's bare skin felt like silk against Clint's own. Her kisses were hot, her flesh scalding, and the heat between her thighs molten.

Rita was full bodied, even more so than it had appeared while she was dressed. She had large breasts, wide hips, perfectly shaped thighs and bottom. He got her to recline on her back, and then began to explore her body with his lips and tongue. Because they had all night, there was no rush. He teased her as much as he could before concentrating his attention on her center.

"Oh God," she whispered, reaching for him, "I'm burning for you."

"That was the plan," he told her.

"With the other girls occupying your time," she told him, pumping his hard cock up and down in her hand, "we have to make this last."

"Oh," he said, "don't worry, it will."

He moved down to press his mouth to her wet center and she gasped.

"Not if you keep doing that!"

"Don't worry," he said, "if it doesn't last, we'll just do it again."

"And again and again, I hope . . ." she breathed, as he dipped his head and went back to his task, lapping up the nectar that was leaking from her like honey . . .

***

When the mayor got to his house there was a man waiting for him on his porch.

"It's about time," the man said. "Where the hell have you been?"

"I was busy," Mayor Hunter said. "Come inside before somebody sees us."

Hunter opened his front door and entered, leaving Mike Duffy to follow.

"Close that door and lock it," Hunter said.

"Right."

Duffy obeyed and followed the mayor inside.

"Whiskey?" Hunter asked.

"Always."

Hunter turned up a couple of lamps, bathing the living room in plenty of light. Then he poured two whiskeys and handed one to Mike Duffy.

"Thanks."

"Have a seat, Mike," Hunter said, seating himself on the sofa.

"How'd the party go?" Duffy asked, sitting in a near-by over-stuffed chair.

"Fine, just fine."

"Then why am I here?" Duffy asked. "I got word you were lookin' for me."

Mayor Hunter wondered how to approach this. He didn't want to get Mike Duffy too worked up.

"You know Clint Adams is in town?"

"Yeah, I heard that," Duffy said. "I'm tryin' to decide what to do about it."

That suited the mayor. At least Duffy wasn't flying off the handle.

"Nothing. You can do nothing . . . for now."

"I figured you'd say that."

"And I figured eventually you wouldn't be able to resist taking a run at him," Hunter said.

"I could do it, too," Duffy said. "You've seen me with a gun."

"I have," Hunter said, "and I'd back you against him, but I need him alive until our competition is over."

"You think he's gonna pick out the girl you want?" Duffy asked.

"I don't know," Hunter said, "but I have to see this out, so you and your partners need to stay away from him."

Duffy laughed.

"My partners ain't gonna go after the Gunsmith, Mr. Mayor," he said. "They'll wait for me to do it."

"And you'll do it when I say so, right?"

"Well . . . I may need some money to keep me goin' until then."

"I thought you might."

There was a desk against the wall. Mayor Hunter stood up, walked to it and took an envelope from the top drawer.

"This should hold you," he said, dropping the envelope on the desk.

Duffy walked to the desk, put down his whiskey glass and picked up the envelope. He tucked it away without counting the contents.

"Okay if I come and see your big competition?" he asked the mayor.

"Sure. It's open to the whole town."

"Then I'll see you there," the gunman said, and left the house.

Hunter hoped he had given the man enough money to keep him occupied gambling, drinking and whoring until the competition was done.

Chapter Eighteen

Clint crawled atop Rita, poking the moist lips of her pussy with his cock. Waves of pleasure had washed over her several times already, and she was so sensitive that just that gentle poke pushed her over the edge yet again.

She was still shuddering when he slid his cock into her, gliding in easily because she was so wet.

"Oh, Jesus," she gasped.

He began to fuck her, slowly at first, then faster and faster as she found his rhythm and was able to match it.

"Oh, yes," she said, her tone husky, "that's it, just like that . . ."

And he kept it up, just like that, until once again she closed her eyes, tensed all over, and then exploded beneath him, as if trying to buck him off. But Clint had ridden many bedroom broncs before, and he stayed with her, sliding his hands beneath to cup her buttocks. He drove himself in and out until he felt his own release boiling up from deep inside him. He could feel it, starting in his legs and working its way up, until finally he let himself explode inside of her . . .

***

"Still feel like you might have made a mistake coming here?"

He was sitting on the edge of the bed, looking for his clothes, which were strewn around the room. She was lying on her back with one leg crossed over a knee. He could see the insides of her thighs, but the prize between them was hidden.

"Not here," he said, indicating her bedroom. "But if you're right, I'm going to be beating off pretty saloon girls over the next few days."

"Most men would love that."

"I like to pick my women out, one by one," he said. "By the way, how long is this contest supposed to take?"

"I'm not sure," she said. "Two or three days. At least, that's all I told Randall I could give him away from my business."

"You're going to close your store for that time?" Clint asked.

"Yes," she said. "I don't trust anyone else to run it. And besides, I have a lot of dresses in the competition. So it's good advertising for me."

He started to dress. When he had his trousers on, he sat to pull on his boots. She rolled over onto her side and leaned on one elbow.

"You've had enough of me tonight?" she asked.

"I do have to get some rest," he told her, "but the key phrase there is 'for tonight.'"

"Oh, I don't know if we'll have another night," she said. "Not with all those girls."

He stood up and strapped on his gun, then leaned over and kissed her. Her body was still giving off intense heat.

"You're talking about girls," he said to her. "I always prefer women."

"When all those soft young bodies start coming out of the woodwork," she said, "we'll see."

"I'll see you tomorrow."

"I don't know how early I'll be getting around," she said, rolling onto her back so he could see everything she had. "You've worn me out."

"Same here," he said, "which is why I'm leaving to get some rest."

He left her bedroom, walked across the living room and out the front door. As he closed the door, he heard something behind him, turned in time to see a shadow running away. He didn't bother to chase after it, since no shots had been fired. But someone had been watching them. He would have to ask both Flatt and Rita who might be watching. And why?

***

When he entered the empty hotel lobby, the middle-aged desk clerk waved at him frantically.

"Mr. Adams," he said, "I've had to chase girls away from your room all night."

"Girls?"

"Saloon girls," the man said. "I recognized some of 'em, like Amy from the Gun Barrel. I guess they must all be in that contest."

"Is anyone up there now?" Clint asked.

"No, sir, I didn't let anybody up."

"Okay, thanks."

"I also got somethin' for ya," the clerk said. He took an envelope from beneath the desk and handed it over.

"Do you know what it is?" Clint asked.

"Not a clue."

"Okay, thanks. Oh, just keep shooing the girls away from my door, okay?"

"Sure, Mr. Adams."

Clint went up to his room, opened the door slowly, and stepped in when he saw that it was empty. He closed the door, then opened the envelope. Inside was a schedule of events. The first was scheduled for 9 a.m.

He placed it on top of the dresser, got undressed, stuck a chair back under the doorknob, and went to sleep.

Chapter Nineteen

The next morning he woke early so he could have a leisurely breakfast before the competition started. Penelope smiled at him when he entered the café.

"Amy said she danced with you last night," she said, coming to his table. "She says you're a good dancer."

"You would've found that out for yourself if you'd been there," he said. "I would've danced with you."

She blushed and asked, "What would you like for breakfast?"

"Well, I don't know how long I'll be busy with this contest, so I better have a big one."

"Leave it to me?" she asked.

"Okay," Clint said. "I'll trust you."

"You won't be disappointed."

She turned and hurried to the kitchen. When she reappeared, she had a pot of coffee and a cup. She poured it for him, then rushed back to the kitchen. She was moving with such enthusiasm that other diners in the place watched her.

Clint drank the coffee. It was as good as he remembered, but it wasn't as good as the Jamaican coffee he'd had.

He was working on a second cup when Penelope returned with a large plate of steak, eggs and spuds. She also set down a basket of warm biscuits.

"Does that look like it'll hold you?" Penelope asked.

"Penny, this looks fine," Clint said. "Thank you."

"I have other tables to take care of," she said, "but I'll be back."

"I'll be here," he promised.

As she saw to her other customers, he tucked into his breakfast. Sex with Rita Mason the night before had resulted in a voracious appetite this morning. By the time she got back around to him, he was on his last cup of coffee, and his final biscuit.

"My God," she said, "you *were* hungry, weren't you?"

"Starving," he said.

"Do you want some more?"

"No, thanks," he said. "I'm full. By the way, who does the cooking, you?"

"Oh no," she said, "I'm just a waitress. I can't cook. That's Charlie. He's amazing with a stove."

"Well, you tell Charlie I said that was a wonderful breakfast."

"Are you going to the competition now?" she asked.

"Yes, it's supposed to start at nine." He looked at the clock on the wall. "Fifteen minutes. Are you going to come and watch your sister compete?"

"No," she said. "I have to work. But I'll be able to stop by tonight, if there's anything going on."

"There will be," he promised. "They've got events planned all day."

He stood up and paid his bill, putting plenty of extra for her on the table.

"That's too much," she told him.

"Not for the kind of service I got," he said. "I'll see you later, Penny."

***

The first event was scheduled to take place in the same ballroom in City Hall where the party had been. As Clint entered, he saw that a makeshift stage had been erected, probably overnight.

"Clint!" Randall Flatt shouted. "Wow, I'm glad you're here. Now I just need our other two judges."

"Isn't the mayor just upstairs?" Clint asked.

"Oh, yeah," Flatt said, "but he'll make his usual late entrance. Have you seen Rita?"

"Not since we left here yesterday," he lied.

"Well," Flatt said, "she better show up."

"I think she will," Clint said. "You know how women are. Maybe she wants to make her own entrance."

"Rita's not that type," Flatt said.

"And what about your wife?" Clint asked. "Will she be coming here?"

"She has to run the store," Flatt said, "so no, she won't."

"Too bad," Clint said. "She should see your success."

"Like I said," Flatt replied, "this is not her cup of tea."

"Is she worried about you and one of the girls?" Clint asked.

"Oh, no, not that," Flatt said. "In fact, I don't think she'd even care."

"Why not?" Clint asked. "If the girls are going to try to sway me, they might also try to sway you."

Flatt hesitated, thinking about what Clint said.

"No, no," he said then, "that's not going to happen."

"Why not?"

"I'm just not the type."

"Men are all the type to be approached by a beautiful girl," Clint said.

"I'm not the type to accept," Flatt said. "I've never been a ladies' man, Clint. I think you can tell that by my wife."

"What's wrong with your wife?" Clint asked. "She's lovely."

"She's a bitch," Flatt said. "Ah, here's Rita."

Chapter Twenty

Rita Mason came walking across the room to them. She was wearing a dress that was not fancy or flashy but was anything but simple. Clint was sure she had made it, herself. It was blue and fit her perfectly.

"You had me worried," Flatt said.

"Why? I told you I'd be here. Good morning, Clint."

"Good morning, Rita."

She looked around.

"Looks like our third judge is late, again."

"Always," Flatt said, "but he wouldn't miss it."

"And the girls?" Rita asked.

"They're all ready."

As they walked people began to file in and take seats in front of the temporary stage.

"Looks like the town's really turning out for you," Rita said.

"Yes," Flatt said, "so far. Excuse me, I have to get the girls ready."

As Flatt left them, Rita moved closer to Clint and said, "My legs are still weak."

"So are mine," Clint said. "And I was so hungry this morning I had a huge breakfast."

"And when you got to your hotel?" she asked. "Did you have company?"

"They tried," Clint said, "but the desk clerk told me he sent them away."

"Oh, too bad."

At that point the mayor entered and began shaking hands all around the room, until he reached Clint and Rita.

"I believe we're supposed to sit up front," he told them. "Shall we?"

"Lead the way, Mr. Mayor," Rita said.

They walked to the front row and sat down.

***

Randall Flatt came out onto the stage and announced the opening of the Miss Dance Hall Competition.

"And here are all our competitors," he said, with a wave of his arm.

The girls filed out of a doorway onto the stage, dressed in their best saloon gowns. There was a lot of color, and lots of skin. The crowd applauded and the men whistled.

The girls all got onto the stage and lined up, facing the audience, so everyone could get a good look at them.

"And now," Flatt announced, "each girl will tell us what they would do if they won. First, Amy, from the Gun Barrel Saloon . . ."

Each girl telling what she would do if she won went on for hours. Clint felt his eyelids getting heavy, and he swore Rita swayed into him, almost falling asleep, herself.

"I'm going to the bar," he said to her. "Anything for you?"

"Only if they have more than beer," she said.

He didn't bother asking the mayor if he wanted anything.

At the bar he said, "A beer, and do you have anything else?"

"Sarsaparilla?" the bartender asked.

"Stronger?"

The bartender looked beneath the bar.

"I seem to have a couple of bottles of red wine."

"That'll do."

While the bartender poured, three men came and surrounded Clint at the bar. He looked them over, saw three burly men in their twenties who—thankfully—were not wearing guns.

"Gents," he said, "I could use a little more room."

"Yer a judge, ain'tcha?" one of them said.

"That's right."

"Well," a second man said, "one of the girls is our sister."

"Is that right?"

"Yep," the third man said, "her name's Nancy. She works at the Red Garter Saloon."

"I haven't been there."

"Well," the first man said, "she's the girl in the middle, in the purple dress."

Clint looked up at the stage and spotted the girl they were talking about.

"Pretty girl," he said.

"Pretty?" the first brother said. "She's beautiful."

"If you say so."

Clint turned and accepted the drinks from the bartender. When he turned to leave the brothers were still in his way.

"Something I can do for you boys?"

"Yeah," the first brother said, "you could see to it that our Nancy wins."

"If she deserves it," he said, "I'll be sure to do that."

"If she don't win," the second brother said, "we ain't gonna be happy."

"Then she better do her best, don't you think?" Clint asked. "Excuse me."

He walked back over to his seat and handed Rita her drink.

"What took so long?" she asked.

"The brothers of one of the girls threatened me," he said.

She looked around.

"Where are they?"

Clint also looked.

"I guess they must've left. Three big burly types in their twenties."

"Sounds like the MacLeod brothers," the mayor said, leaning over.

"Apparently the girl in the middle, Nancy, is their sister."

"Right," the mayor said, "she works at the Red Garter."

"That dump?" Rita asked.

"But she is a pretty girl," Clint said, looking up at the one in the purple dress.

"But that dress!" Rita said.

"I assume you didn't make it?" Clint asked.

"Please!" she said, with distaste. "Look at that hem. And the seams!"

"How many of these dresses did you actually make?" Clint asked.

"About half," she said.

"That beer looks good," the mayor said. "I guess you need a drink to get through this, huh?"

Clint hadn't taken a sip yet, so he handed it to the mayor and said, "Be my guest."

Chapter Twenty-One

Eventually, the girls all took a bow and filed back off the stage. Amy saw Clint and waved to him. He waved back. The only other saloon girl he knew was Nancy, because her 3 hulking brothers had pointed her out.

"We'll see you all at the three o'clock segment!" Randall Flatt announced.

"Well," the mayor said, "back to the office." He handed Clint the empty beer mug. "Thank you for the drink."

He stood, nodded to Rita, and left with the filing out crowd.

Randall Flatt came down off the stage and joined them.

"So, what did you think?" he asked.

"Lots of pretty girls," Clint said.

"I know it was a little boring, but it'll get better," he said.

"What are they going to do this afternoon?" Rita asked.

"Didn't you read the schedule I sent over?" Flatt asked.

"Uh, no, I didn't get the chance."

"The girls are going to show off their serving skills," Clint said.

"Ah, you read it," Flatt said.

"Yes, I did."

"Good, Good."

"And what are you going to do between now and three?" Clint asked.

"I have lots to do," Flatt said, "but can I ask you a favor?"

"Sure," Clint said. "What is it?"

"Will you go and talk to Adele for me?"

"You want Clint to go and see your wife?" Rita asked.

"Yes," Flatt said, "she needs to be told what I'm doing."

"You didn't tell her this morning when you left the house?" Clint asked.

"She was asleep."

"And she hasn't read the schedule?" Rita asked.

"She couldn't care less," Flatt said, "but I can't have her expecting me at the store when I won't be there all day. Will you do that for me?"

"Of course," Clint said. "I'll go and talk to her right away."

"Then I might as well go to my store," Rita said.

"I thought you were closed," Clint said.

"I am, but I have some work I can do in the back."

"Then I'll walk you."

"Thank you," she said. "You're very gallant."

"I'll see you both later, then," Flatt said, and rushed off.

"I thought we'd go to my house," Rita said, as they left the building.

"That's probably not a good idea in the daylight," he told her.

"Maybe not," she said.

"What did you think of the girls?" Clint asked, as they headed for her store.

"Should we be talking about that?" she asked. "We might influence each other's opinions."

"Good point," he said. "Let's make up our own mind."

When they reached her store, he waited while she unlocked the door, and when she went in, he continued on to the mercantile.

***

As he entered, Adele Flatt was tending to a couple of male customers.

"I'll be with you in a minute," she told Clint.

"No hurry," he assured her.

She finished up with the two men, who seemed to be putting in an order for their boss, a local rancher.

"Don't know why he couldn't do this himself," one of them complained on the way out.

"He's at City Hall lookin' at pretty girls," the other said.

"I know," the first man said. "That's where I wanna be."

"Idiots," Adele Flatt said.

"I'm sorry?"

"Complaining because they can't be watching that stupid contest my husband's putting on," she said. "Why sit and look at women when you could be with one?"

"Well, I—"

"I'm sure you've been with your share of women," she said. "Rather than sitting watching them strut around."

She walked past him, closed the door, locked it and turned the sign around in the window to read CLOSED.

"Mrs. Flatt—"

"Just call me Adele," she said, turning to face him.

"Adele," he said, "your husband sent me over here—"

"That was very nice of him," she said. "Would you come into the storeroom with me?"

She didn't wait for an answer, just walked past him and through a doorway.

"Hurry!" she called out, when he didn't move right away.

His hesitation had given her just enough time to get naked before he went through the doorway, saw her and stopped short.

Chapter Twenty-Two

"Mrs. Flatt—" he started.

"Adele," she said, putting her hands on her hips.

Rita Mason had been full-bodied. This woman was lush, with acres of flesh that flowed into curves everywhere. It was amazing how some women's clothes buried the body beneath. He had originally thought Adele a handsome woman, but now his body was reacting to her raw sexuality.

"Don't you think, considering the circumstances we're in, you could call me Adele?"

"Adele . . . you're married—"

"Are you gonna tell me the Gunsmith doesn't sleep with married women?" she asked. "I would think you'd do anything you wanted to."

"But I know your husband," Clint said, "and I'm practically working for him."

"You're not friends and he's not paying you," she said, staring at his crotch. "And you can't tell me you're not reacting."

Her large breasts, topped with dark brown nipples, were pointing right at him. He found himself wondering what they would feel like in his mouth and knew it would only take a few steps to find out.

"Jesus, Adele . . ."

"Ah," she said, smiling, "there's the reaction I wanted."

***

Randall Flatt knocked on the door and it was opened quickly by Nancy MacLeod.

"Get in here!" she said, grabbing him and pulling him inside.

Nancy was a very pretty girl in her mid-20s, with long, tawny hair and hard, high breasts. She was still wearing the purple dress she had worn on stage.

"Why would you come here like this?" she demanded.

"Your brothers."

She rolled her violet eyes.

"What did they do now?" Her brothers were triplets, a couple of years younger than she was. And between them they didn't have a working brain.

"They threatened Clint Adams," he said, "if he didn't see to it that you won."

"That ain't his job," she said, "it's yours, remember?"

"I do, Nancy," Flatt said, "but they're gonna get themselves killed threatening the Gunsmith. And it won't be good for the competition."

"Look," she said, "the only thing that won't be good for this competition is if I don't win."

"I know that!"

"And you knew it the first time you came here," she said, reaching down to cup his crotch, "and I gave you a suck."

"I never asked you to do that!" he exclaimed, even as his cock got hard from her touch.

She rubbed him through his pants and said, "You asked like you're askin' now."

Thankfully, Nancy had her own little house away from the main part of town. She left her family home, not wanting to share it with her parents and her brothers. This house had been available, and even though she didn't make a lot of money at the Red Garter, she had managed to do what she had to do to afford it—which meant also giving the banker a suck.

But even though the house was off the beaten path, there was always a chance somebody might see Randall Flatt there.

"You got to get out of here," she said. "I gotta get ready for the next part, and that means a bath."

At the mention that she was going to take a bath, the vision of her naked and wet came to him, and he almost messed his pants.

"Oh, okay," she said, "I see. Well, let's make this quick."

She hurriedly yanked his trousers and underwear down around his ankles and took his painfully hard penis into her mouth. And quick it was, which was why she didn't much mind doing it. A few sucks, and a tickle of his balls, and he shot his load into her mouth. It was a small price to pay.

She stood up and wiped the corners of her mouth with her fingers.

"How was that?" she asked. "Good enough?"

"Oh, God," he said, pulling up his trousers and yanking on his belt. "I didn't ask for that, Nancy. I ain't forcing you!"

"No, you ain't," she said, "but you ain't pushin' me away neither, Randall. Now get outta here before somebody comes along."

"Somebody . . . like who?"

"Like somebody else I might hafta suck."

His eyes went wide.

"You do this for other men?"

"And they pay me!" she said, quickly. "You wanna pay me?"

"Jesus," he started, "I ain't never even been to a whorehouse—"

"And you ain't been now," she said. "This ain't a whorehouse. I ain't exactly a who—look, just get outta here! And make sure I win, if ya don't want your wife to find out what we did here—twice!"

"Jesus," he said, and ran for the door.

Chapter Twenty-Three

What Clint and Adele Flatt were doing in her back room was taking much longer than what Nancy MacLeod and Randall Flatt had just done.

It was an odd last name for this woman to have, because there was absolutely nothing flat about her, at all. At the age of 39 or 40, she had all the rolling curves a woman who was built to be bedded was meant to have.

Clint still had it in his head to back out of the room and get out of that store, but for some reason his legs would not move. That gave the naked woman time to approach him and start to undress him.

"I know a man like you won't want to be far from his gun, so here," she said, pointing to a peg on the wall, "hang it right there."

He did so and then she started on his trousers. When she had them around his ankles, and his cock was poking straight out at her, she got down on her knees and started to suck it in long, loving, wet strokes. As she did so he leaned over, ran his hands down her naked back to her generous butt, then slid one hand between her thighs and began to stroke her wet pussy like that.

She groaned, tried to spread her thighs for him without letting him slip from her hot mouth. While she got him rock hard, he got her soaking wet. After only a short time, they were ready for each other.

He slid his hands beneath her arms, lifted her up from her knees, set her down on the top of a nearby crate, spread her thighs, and poked his hard cock into her wet depths.

"Oh God!" she gasped, "Oh my!" her eyes going wide. "Oh Jesus." She reached out and put her hands on his shoulders as he started to move in and out of her. At the same time he finally got those nipples into his mouth, and worked them with his teeth and lips. "I've had sex before, but . . . it's never felt like this!"

"It never feels the same," he said, between thrusts. "People are different."

"No, no," she said, gasping, "you don't understand. With my husband it's never . . . been anything close to . . . to this."

"Well," he said, "it gets better."

Her eyes widened.

"It can't!"

He grinned, decided to give her as much as he could, since she had been so demanding, not to mention threatening.

He withdrew his cock from her, knelt down in front of her and pressed his face to her . . .

***

"You were right," she said, after the spasm ceased and she was able to stop trying to muffle her screams, "it did get better."

"I told you."

"My God," she said, pulling on her dress. "If I didn't have to re-open the store, I wouldn't let you leave."

"I have to get back to the competition," he said, "and let your husband know I delivered his message."

"I think you delivered a little more than that," she laughed.

He buttoned his shirt, tucked it in and strapped on his gunbelt. Together, they walked back into the store.

"Wow," she said, "I feel so good. For the first time in . . . months I don't feel angry."

"That's good, right?"

"I don't know," she said. "After all, I'm still married to Flatt."

"I've got to go," Clint said.

"On your way out will you turn the sign to open?" she asked. "And, by the way, thanks."

Chapter Twenty-Four

The sex had been good.

The feeling after was not.

He felt bad about having sex with Randall Flatt's wife, but after all, it was Flatt who had sent him to his unsatisfied, angry wife. Maybe the man had known what he was doing?

But he sure as hell wasn't going to tell the man he had slept with his wife. He'd just start by telling him he delivered his message, and the woman had reacted . . . calmly. After all, she had been pretty calm when he left.

He didn't go looking for Randall Flatt, though. He'd see him soon enough at the next Miss Dance Hall event. Instead, he stopped in a small saloon he had not yet been to for a much-needed beer.

The place was mostly empty, with only a few drinkers staring into their beer or whiskey.

"There ya go," the bartender said, setting a beer in front of him.

"Thanks."

The thin man set his elbow on the bar and said, "You're one of the contest judges, ain'tcha?"

Clint took a moment to sip his beer before responding.

"You know, we got a girl in that contest."

"Is that right?"

"Her name's Greta? Do you remember her?"

"Hmm," Clint said, making a show of thinking about it, "Greta, of . . ."

"The Rawhide Saloon," the bartender said, proudly.

"The Rawhide Saloon," Clint repeated.

"She was wearin' green" the bartender said, with a smile.

"Green . . . oh, and she has red hair?" Clint asked.

"That's her! You do remember."

Actually, he did. She was a tall, slender redhead with regal bearing. He was surprised she came from a small place like the Rawhide.

"I remember," Clint said. "Greta."

"Do you think she has a chance?"

"They all have a chance," Clint replied.

"Tell me," the bartender asked, "is there any way we could make sure she has a, uh, better chance?"

"I'm afraid not," Clint said. "She's going to have to win it on her own merit."

"Oh." The bartender stood up straight and looked unhappy. "Four bits."

"For what?" Clint asked.

"The beer," the bartender said, "Four bits."

"That's kind of steep, isn't it?" Clint asked.

"It could be on the house," the bartender said.

"That's okay," Clint said. "I'll pay." He dug out four bits and set it on the bar.

"If you change your mind—" the bartender said.

"Why don't we just let the girl see if she can win on her own, huh?" Clint asked.

"Why?" the man asked. "We all know the girl who works at the biggest saloon will win."

"How do we know that?"

"Why don't you ask the mayor?"

"Maybe I'll do that." Clint headed for the door, then stopped. "Which saloon in the biggest in town?"

"That'd be the Silver Dollar," the bartender said. "It's just a bit bigger than the Gun Barrel."

"I see," Clint said. "Thanks."

He left the Rawhide and went to find the Silver Dollar.

***

Clint was surprised that he had not found his way to the Silver Dollar yet—especially when he saw it. It was right on the corner intersection of two streets, but one them was not Main Street. Clint simply had not walked by it before, not even on his walk around town.

He entered, found it busy even at that early hour. He walked to the bar, where there was still plenty of room.

"Beer, please," he told the bartender.

"Comin' up."

When he brought it Clint asked, "How come this place isn't more toward the center of town?"

"When the boss opened it, he wanted to have the biggest place in town," the bartender said. "There wasn't a building on Main Street bigger than this one, so he put it here."

"And how's business?"

"It's great," the bartender said. "The only place that can compete is the Gun Barrel."

"And do you have any girls in this contest that's going on?"

"Oh yeah," the bartender said, "We have three."

Clint wondered if he hadn't been paying attention that morning when three girls said they were from the Silver Dollar Saloon?

"We got Lisa, Milly and Kitty."

"Are they pretty?"

"They sure are!"

Clint raised his glass.

"Then I'll drink to their good luck."

The bartender poured himself a shot of whiskey and said, "Me, too!"

Chapter Twenty-Five

Clint still had an hour before he had to return to the competition's next event. He was assuming it would also take place in the City Hall building. He would have gone to see Rita at her store, but he was concerned that she would smell Adele Flatt on him. Women could do that. So he decided to go to his hotel room and wash up—thoroughly.

In his room he stripped off his shirt, washed his hands, face, neck and chest, then put another shirt on. Because he was judging a contest of beautiful women, he had thought to buy extra shirts for the event. Now he was going to have to get them cleaned. He wondered if there was a Chinese laundry in town?

Freshened, he went downstairs and asked the clerk about the laundry.

"Ling-Ling's is two blocks down, and around the corner," the clerk said. "But if you have something, we can take it to them. And when it's cleaned, bring it back."

"That'd be good," Clint said. "Upstairs. On the bed, are some shirts."

"I'll have them picked up," the middle-aged clerk said.

"And if anything else is missing from my room," Clint said, "I'll come and talk to you about it."

"That won't happen, sir," the clerk said. "We're very honest here."

"That's good to know."

Clint went out, satisfied that his shirts would be back and clean when he returned. As he was walking toward City Hall, he saw a man coming his way with purposeful stride. As he got closer, he recognized him as the hostler who was caring for Eclipse.

"There you are!" the man shouted. "I knew I'd find ya."

"Is there something wrong with my horse?" Clint asked.

"No, no, he's fine," the man said. "That horse is as strong as an ox."

"Then why are you looking for me?"

"I wanted to see what ya thought of my Betty this mornin'," the man said. "Ain't she a beauty?"

"Betty," Clint said. "What saloon does she work in?"

"She's from the Gun Barrel."

"Ah, where Amy works."

"Yeah, but Amy ain't the beauty my Betty is," the man said, "You saw her."

"I did," Clint said, even though he couldn't remember a Betty. "Very pretty girl."

"You think she's got a chance ta win?" the man asked.

"They all have a chance . . ." Clint said.

"Yeah, but—"

"What's your name?" Clint asked.

"Me? Folks call me Horseshoe."

"Horseshoe," Clint said, "I can't talk to you about my judging. Okay?"

"Oh, sure," the man said, "I understand that. But re-member . . . I've got your horse."

Clint stared at the man.

"Are you threatening my horse if I don't let your daughter win?"

The man looked surprised.

"No, no," he said, raising his hands, "Jesus, I'm sorry I said that. I'd never harm a horse—especially not yours."

"Horseshoe," Clint said, "if anything happens to that horse—"

"Don't worry," the hostler said, "I'll take good care of him, no matter what else happens. I swear!"

Clint poked him in the chest.

"See to it that you do!"

As he walked away Horseshoe called out, "But my Betty's a pretty gal, right?"

Clint waved without turning around.

***

When he reached the City Hall building and walked into the ballroom, he found it empty. The temporary stage had been taken down.

"Where is everybody?"

He turned to look at Rita, who appeared to be very confused.

"That's what I was wondering."

"Randall didn't tell you?" Clint asked.

"No," she said. "He didn't tell you?"

"No."

"Maybe the mayor knows," Rita offered.

"We could go up and ask him," Clint offered.

"Or," Rita suggested, "we could just wait for him to come down."

"Good idea," Clint said.

"So what did you do this afternoon?"

"I went back to my hotel," Clint said, "got washed up—oh, and I had a conversation with this fella named Horseshoe?" It was only a lie by omission, because he did go back to his room, he just did something before that he didn't what her to know about.

"Runs the livery, right?"

"Yep," Clint said. "He threatened my horse if I didn't let his daughter win."

"His daughter?" Rita asked, frowning again. "Which one is his daughter?"

"Betty?" Clint said. "From the Gun Barrel?"

"I think she's a pretty girl," Rita said.

"That's what I told him," Clint said, "but they're all pretty girls, or they wouldn't be competing."

"That's true."

Clint and Rita decided to go outside and wait for the mayor to come out of his office. But when the front door opened it was the mayor's assistant, a bookish man named Edward Lowry, who came out.

"Edward," Rita said, "where's the mayor?"

"He's out at the competition," Lowry said.

"We don't know where that is," Clint said.

"It was on the schedule," Lowry told them.

"I still haven't read it," Rita said.

"I can take mine out of my pocket," Clint said, "but why don't you just tell us where it is?"

"I can do better than that," Lowry said. "I'm on my way over there. I'll take you."

Chapter Twenty-Six

They followed Lowry through town, and as they approached an open area, they were joined by others going the same way.

"Where are we going?" Rita asked.

"There's a clearing just outside of town where carnival shows and the circus sets up when they come to town," Lowry said. "That's where they've erected a tent."

Clint and Rita looked at each other. Neither of them knew anything about a tent outside of town. Clint didn't even think it said anything about it on his schedule.

"I can't believe Randall forgot to tell us where to go," Rita said. "He's been so organized."

"It might have just slipped his mind this morning," Clint suggested.

Lowry stopped walking.

"The mayor should be in the tent," he said.

"Aren't you coming in?" Rita asked.

"I have other things to do," the small man said. "The mayor doesn't expect me to attend this . . . this competition. But you enjoy it."

Lowry walked away, a look on his face as if he had smelled something bad.

"Obviously he's not in favor of this competition," Rita said.

"It looks like the town is turning out for it," Clint said, as people walked past them in droves.

"When there's a circus here," she said, "or a carnival, they also turn out."

"I hope they're not expecting clowns this time," Clint said.

"We better go in."

They approached the tent, and as they entered, Randall Flatt came running over.

"There you are!"

"Are we on time?" Clint asked.

"Just barely."

"Then don't worry so much," Clint told him, putting his hand on the man's shoulder.

"Okay, you're right," Flatt said. "Oh, did you give my wife my message?"

"I did."

"How did she take it?"

"She took it as well as could be expected," Clint said, carefully.

"Ah, I'll pay for it tonight," Flatt said. "We better get started. Where's the mayor?"

"His man Lowry told us he was in here," Clint said.

"Well, he's not," Flatt said. "Now he's gonna make us have a late start! You two better go in front and sit. I'll find him."

***

Back at City Hall, Lowry entered the building and found the mayor waiting for him downstairs.

"How's it going?" Hunter asked.

"The tent's filling up with townspeople," Lowry assured him.

"And is the Gunsmith there?"

"He is."

"All right," Mayor Hunter said, "then it's time for Mike Duffy and his men to make their move. You go and tell them, and I'll go to the tent."

"Yessir," Lowry said. "Uh, sir, do you think this is really the right thing to do?"

"Not only is it right," Hunter said, "it's necessary. Now go!"

"Yessir," Lowry said. "I'm going."

They left the City Hall building together, Lowry going one way, and the mayor the other.

Chapter Twenty-Seven

The mayor arrived just in time for the festivities to start. Randall Flatt, relieved, took his place on the temporary stage. Behind him was a table and chairs, like you would see in a saloon. Off to the right, a bar.

"Oh, Jesus," Clint said, as he realized what was going to happen.

"What?" Rita asked.

"Watch."

"Thank you all for coming," Flatt said. "Now you'll get a chance to see our girls in action. This is what they do every night, and the skill they do it with. First you'll see Amy, from the Gun Barrel."

Amy came out in her gown, curtsied to all the applause, then went to the bar, where a man had taken his place behind it, playing the bartender. Two other men took seats at the table. The bartender handed Amy a tray laden with drinks. She turned and carried it to the table with one hand, even threw in a pirouette as one of men made a grab for her, then set the drinks down on the table. That done she turned to the audience and spread her hands. It took a moment for the audience to realize it was time to applaud.

"Oh, no" Rita said.

"Oh, yes," Clint said. "We're going to have to watch each girl do that."

Rita pressed her fingers to her forehead and closed her eyes.

"Twelve times?" she said.

"Next," Flatt said, as Amy left the stage, "Betty, from the Gun Barrel."

***

It took hours for Flatt to introduce each girl, for the girl to bow or curtsy, then collect her tray from the mock bar and deliver the drinks while dancing across the stage and evading grasping male hands.

Rita sighed more than once and rolled her eyes.

Under other circumstances, Clint might have enjoyed watching pretty girls prance across a stage, but on this day, it was just too boring for words. One time he looked over at the mayor, who seemed to be dozing.

At one point Clint felt that the stares of the crowd were not on the girls, but on him. Apparently, word had gone around about who he was. The mayor noticed his glances and leaned over.

"You don't think these people are all here to see girls, do you?" Hunter asked. "They're here to see if you're going to shoot anyone."

"Well," Clint said, "if that's the case, they'll be disappointed."

The last girl to go was Nancy MacLeod, from the Red Garter Saloon. As her three brothers had said, she was very pretty, and moved very confidently with the tray of drinks balanced on her hand.

"Wonderful dexterity on that girl," the mayor commented.

Clint figured that was because he happened to be awake when she walked across the stage.

"Ladies and gentlemen," Randall Flatt said, "that was all of our girls. The judges will now have to consult with each other and decide who did the best this time around. Our next event will actually be the elimination of four of the girls. We will do that back here tonight at nine. That is two hours from now."

"I'm starving!" Rita said, as they filed out. "Let's consult over a steak."

"I have to go back to my office," the mayor said. "I'll merely write down the names of the girls I think should be eliminated. Then we'll meet back here at oh, let's say ten to nine to compare?"

"That's fine," Clint said. "See you then, Mr. Mayor."

As the mayor hurried out the door Clint looked at Rita and said, "The Steakhouse?"

"My thoughts exactly."

***

They went to the Redwind Steakhouse and, since it was after supper time, were able to get a table against the back wall with no trouble.

"I guess the rest of the people from the tent are going home to eat," Clint said, looking around.

"And what about the mayor?" Rita said. "Where was he rushing off to?"

"He looks like a man who misses a lot of meals," Clint observed.

"I'm sure he keeps himself busy."

They both ordered steak dinners and mugs of beer.

"What are your plans for tonight?" she asked.

"I don't know," Clint said. "I thought I'd visit a couple of the saloons."

"You haven't seen enough saloon girls for one day?"

"I was thinking about playing some poker."

"Well," she said, "if you get tired of girls and poker, come and see me."

"It might be late."

"Wake me," she said, "I'm sure you'll make it worth my time."

The waiter came with their plates, asked if they wanted anything else.

"Yes," Rita said, "but it's not something I can get here."

Chapter Twenty-Eight

"Was it done?" the mayor asked Lowry when he got back to his office. "I didn't hear anything in the street."

"No sir, it was not."

"Why not?"

"According to Duffy," Lowry said, "there was sheriff's deputies there."

"Shit!" the mayor said. "Of all the times for those useless deputies to be in the way."

"Yes sir."

"All right." Mayor Hunter sat back in his chair and fumed silently for several minutes while Lowry waited. If his boss hadn't promised to take him along when he moved onward and upward in politics, he certainly would not have gone for any of this.

"All right," the mayor said, again. "Get me the sheriff."

"Now, or in the morning?" Lowry asked. "I mean, it's late—"

"Now!" the mayor snapped. "I'm here, you're here . . . get him here now!"

"Yes sir."

***

The long-time sheriff of Redwind, Texas was a man named Charles Ritch—otherwise known as Charlie, or Chuck Ritch. The reason he was the long-time sheriff was because he cooperated with the long-time mayor. When he got the word that Mayor Hunter wanted to see him, he was there in minutes. After all, Chuck Ritch was on the wrong side of 60, and rarely left his office.

"Mr. Mayor," he said, as he entered the office.

"Shut up and sit down, Sheriff," Hunter said.

"What's the problem, Hubert?" Sheriff Ritch asked.

"The problem is your deputies," Hunter said.

"What did the boys do?" Ritch asked.

"They were in the way today, that's what they did," Hunter said. "Why do you have them both out doing rounds during the day?"

"To keep law and order, sir," Ritch said. "Ain't that their job?"

"Charlie," Hunter said, "for the next few days, I don't want to see your deputies anywhere near town. And I certainly don't want to see them near the bank. You got that?"

"The bank?" Ritch asked. "Which bank. We got three of 'em, Mayor."

"Any of them!" Hunter snapped. "You got me?"

"I got ya, sir," Ritch said. "But what do I tell 'em? My boys are real enthusiastic about upholdin' the law."

"Tell them to go fishing," Hunter said. "I don't want people here for the Miss Dance Hall contest to see them. That's what you tell them. You get me?"

"I get it, Hubie, I get it."

"Now get out, Charlie," Hunter said. "Go and get it done."

Charlie Ritch stood up and rushed from the office as fast as his bandy little legs could take him—all five feet four inches of him.

Lowry came into the office right after that.

"Any more problems, Edward?" Hunter asked him.

"Not that I know of Mr. Mayor," Lowry said. "I just don't know exactly why the Gunsmith is here."

"The Gunsmith was Flatt's idea, goddamnit," Hunter said. "I let him run with the contest, and he wanted a judge with a name."

"But isn't it dangerous having him here?" Lowry asked.

"Maybe it would be for somebody else," Hunter said. "But not for somebody as smart as I am. I'm going to use everything I have at my disposal to make this work."

"I hope that you do, sir," Lowry said. "Do you need me anymore tonight?"

"No, Edward," Hunter said. "Go home."

"Yes, sir. Thank you, sir.

Lowry started to leave, but stopped short in the doorway and turned back.

"What is it?" Hunter asked.

"Uh, sir, there's someone here to see you."

"Who?"

"It's Mike Duffy, sir."

"Jesus!" Hunter said. "Send him in and go home, Edward."

"Yes, sir."

By the time Duffy came through the door, Hunter had two glasses of whiskey on his desk, one in front of him, and one on the other side.

"What is it, Duffy?" he asked.

The gunman walked to the desk, sat and picked up the whiskey glass. He sipped from it before answering.

"We were ready today, Mr. Mayor," Mike Duffy said. "I just want you to know. We probably could've gone ahead, but we would've had to kill two deputies."

"I'm almost sorry you didn't," Hunter said.

"Well, we can do that tomorrow—"

"No, no," Hunter said, hurriedly, "don't kill anybody! Just wait. I told the sheriff to get his men off the street."

"Then we can go ahead?"

"You've got two days," Hunter said. "Just get it done while the competition is going on. That's the key."

"Yes, sir. And what about the Gunsmith?"

"When this job is done," Hunter said, "what you do about the Gunsmith will be up to you."

Mike Duffy finished his whiskey, said, "Yes, sir," and left the office.

Mayor Hunter poured himself another glass of whiskey. He had been filling his war chest for a run at Washington for years now, and the time was almost here. He just couldn't afford for anything to go wrong, because if it worked here, it would also work in Fort Worth.

He took another drink and settled down to make his list of girls who should be eliminated.

Chapter Twenty-Nine

Clint and Rita spent the time together, but not in bed. If they had done that, they might never have gotten back to the tent.

They discussed the contest, and thought they knew who should be eliminated, depending on what the mayor's list looked like.

When they reentered the tent at a quarter to 9, they were surprised to see the mayor sitting in his seat.

"Mr. Mayor," Clint said.

"Mr. Adams," Hunter said. "Here's my list."

He handed it to Clint, who showed it to Rita. Surprisingly they had all settled on the same 4 girls.

"Well," Rita said, "we're in agreement."

"Good," the mayor said.

Randall Flatt came over and said, "Glad my judges are all here early. Have you made your decision?"

"We have," the mayor said, and handed Flatt his written list.

"Is this who you all agree on?" Flatt asked.

"It is," Clint said, and Rita nodded.

"Fine."

Flatt went and got on stage while people were still filing in. After the interminable time spent there earlier in the day, Clint was surprised that most of the people seemed to be returning.

"Ladies and gentlemen," Flatt announced, "the judges have decided which girls should be eliminated. As I call a girl's name she'll come on stage. When we have eight, the other four will be sent home. Ready?"

People applauded.

Flatt began to read off names, starting with Amy. By the time he got to the 7th[th] girl, Nancy MacLeod had not yet been called. Neither had Betty, the hostler's daughter. Clint turned, saw the MacLeod brothers in the back of the tent. He noticed that today they were wearing guns.

"Those boys in the back aren't going to be happy when he reads the last name," Clint said to Rita.

She turned to look and see who he meant, then said, "They're just idiots."

"I know," Clint said, "but they're going to be unhappy idiots."

"Too bad for them."

She turned back around and looked up at the stage.

Flatt called out the last girl's name, and as she came up to join the others, Clint saw both Betty and Nancy react from the floor. Betty started to cry, but Nancy's face darkened and she glared at the three judges,

While the crowd applauded, the MacLeod brothers booed from the back.

Flatt allowed the girls to bow or curtsey, whichever they preferred, and then announced, "Ladies and gents, these are our 8 remaining competitors."

As the applause died down Flatt called out, "Tomorrow morning at nine o'clock, right here! We will eliminate four more girls. Good-night!"

People stood up and started to file out. Clint noticed the MacLeod boys stepped aside to allow everyone to pass.

"Mr. Mayor," Clint aid, "I think you might need an escort. The MacLeod boys are not too happy."

"That's okay," Hunter said, standing. "I appreciate the offer, but they won't touch me. I'm the Mayor. See you two tomorrow."

Hunter followed the last of the audience out of the tent, leaving only Clint, Rita, and the MacLeod boys.

And Nancy and Randall Flatt on stage, where she had charged from the floor.

"You sonofabitch!" Nancy said, and slapped Flatt across the face.

"It wasn't my fault, Nancy," he said. "It's the judge's decision."

She glared down at Clint and Rita.

"Don't be upset, girl," Rita said. "You knew it was a competition."

"My brothers expected me to fare better than this," she complained. "Now I've disappointed them."

"I'm sure they'll understand," Rita told her. "Come down from there and I'll walk you out. Why don't we go to my store? Maybe I have a dress that will make you feel better."

"Well," Nancy said, "A dress from your store would be nice."

"Come along." Rita put her hand out to help the girl down from the stage, and the two of them walked out past her brothers.

"I guess that's it for tonight," Clint said to Flatt who, for some reason, looked nervous. Clint had no idea that the man had been worried about what Nancy would say. "Let's go get a beer."

Flatt nodded and stepped down from the stage. As he and Clint headed for the flap of the tent, the MacLeod brothers blocked their way.

"Just a minute," one of them said. "we told you what'd happen if our sister didn't win."

Clint stopped, and put a hand out to also stop Flatt.

"I forget," Clint said. "Maybe you should remind me."

Chapter Thirty

"You boys better get out of here before I send for the sheriff," Flatt threatened.

The brothers laughed.

"The sheriff never comes out of his office, and the two deputies have gone fishin'," one said.

"I see you've got guns today," Clint said. "That means I need your names."

"Why?" one asked.

"Because I never kill a man without knowing his name."

"I'm Pete, this is Ben and Dan."

"You idiot!" Ben said.

"What?"

"If he didn't know our names, maybe he wouldn't kill us," Ben said.

"He ain't gonna kill us," Pete said. "Not over some silly contest."

"If it's a silly contest," Clint asked, "then what are we all doing here?"

"Nancy wanted to win," Dan said. "That's good enough for me."

"A good enough reason to get killed?" Clint asked.

"This is the Gunsmith, boys," Flatt said. "Are you sure you want to go up against him with guns?"

"We'd rather do it with fists," Pete said, "but he's afraid."

"Is that all it'll take?" Clint asked. "If I fight you and win, this is over?"

Pete laughed.

"When you fight us and take a beatin', it'll be over," he said.

"All three of you?" Clint asked. "That's what it'll take to beat me?"

"Any one of us can give you a beatin'," Pete said.

"Well then," Clint said, "why not you?"

"Yeah, go ahead, Pete," Ben said. "Give him a lickin'."

"What about your gun?" Pete asked.

"I say we all take off our gun belts," Clint said, "so there are no accidents."

"That suits me," Pete said.

"Me, too," Ben said.

"Let's get 'em off," Dan said.

Clint looked at Flatt.

"Will you hold my gun?"

"Well . . . sure," Flatt said. "But . . . are you sure? These are big boys."

"But boys nevertheless," Clint said, unbuckling his belt. "Hold this, but stay close so I can reach it if I need to."

"I get it."

The MacLeod's unbuckled their guns and put the belts aside, on chairs.

"Lemme do it, Pete!" Ben said.

"Naw," Pete said, "I'm the oldest."

"Only by a minute," Ben complained.

That was when Clint realized that the brothers were triplets. They didn't look identical, but enough alike that anyone would know they were brothers.

"Are you sure about this?" Flatt asked. "Why don't you just draw your gun and shoot them?"

"If it comes to that, I will," Clint said, "but not in cold blood. Just stay close, though, in case they go for their guns."

Flatt nodded nervously.

"Well?" Clint asked.

"You in a hurry for a lickin'?" Pete asked.

"I'm in a hurry to get something to eat," Clint said.

"You ain't gonna have no teeth to chew with," Pete said, rolling up his sleeves.

"We'll see about that," Clint said.

Clint put his hands up and took a boxer's stance. He had refereed many boxing matches, and had been in the ring a few times, himself. He decided he might as well try this tactic first.

The burly Pete came in swinging wildly, and Clint was able to sidestep his swings and pepper the man with left jabs. He hit him in the face three times, and the 4th time he let him slide by, and then hit him with a hard right behind the ear. The young man went down on his face.

"That's it," Flatt said. "It's over."

"No it ain't," Ben said, with a grin. "My turn."

Flatt looked at Clint, who simply nodded.

"Come on, then," Clint said to Ben.

The second triplet had a different plan. He wasn't going to box, he was going to wrestle. He spread his arms wide and charged Clint. Clint was able to spin away, but couldn't throw a punch. Ben turned and came at him again like a bull, only quicker. This time as Clint ducked away, he got hit by Ben's big shoulder. It didn't knock him over but drove some of the air from his lungs.

"Get 'im Ben!" Dan shouted.

Ben turned and charged again. This time, instead of trying to dodge the man, Clint charged right at him. They collided, and Ben tried to wrap his arms around Clint.

Clint turned to Dan, who was looking down at his two brothers with dismay all over his face.

"Are you next?" he asked.

Dan looked over at his gun, on a nearby chair.

"Don't even think about it," Clint said. "Just help your brothers up and get out. It's all over."

Dan licked his lips, then leaned over to help first Pete, and then Ben to his feet. For a moment, Clint thought they were considering charging him all at once, but in the end they picked up their gunbelts and Pete led the way out of the tent—still unsteady on his feet from Clint's near rabbit punch.

"Wow," Flatt said, handing Clint his gun, "that was amazing—I didn't think you had a chance against those bigger, younger men."

"When they're that size, they tend to rely on it way too much," Clint said, strapping the gun back on. "Can I buy you a beer?"

"You sure can."

"How about the Gun Barrel?" Clint suggested. "We eliminated Betty, but they're still in the running with Amy."

"Good thinkin'," Flatt said, and followed Clint from the tent.

Chapter Thirty-One

The Gun Barrel was busy, all the tables full, the girls running with drinks, and the bar a bevy of activity.

"No room at the inn," Flatt observed.

But at that moment Amy came walking over.

"Do you gents want a table?" she asked.

"Back at work so soon after the competition?" Clint asked.

"I still have to make a livin', don't I?" she asked.

"Well, we just need some room at the bar, not a table," Clint said.

"Come with me, then," Amy said. "I'll take care of it."

They followed her to the bar, where she elbowed them enough room for the two of them. The men she poked turned, ready to be angry, but when they saw her pretty face they moved aside, not wanting to offend a pretty girl.

"There you are," she said. "Do I know how to do my job, or not?"

Clint realized she was still performing for one of the contest judges. He decided to toss her a bone.

"You sure do, Amy," Clint said. "I'm going to tell your sister that."

"I wish you would," Amy said, and flounced away.

"Her sister?" Flatt asked.

"She's a waitress at a small café near my hotel," Clint told him.

"Ah, I think I know the place."

"Real good food," Clint said. He waved for the bartender and ordered two beers. When they came he handed Flatt one of them.

"So how do you think the competition is going?" Flatt asked.

"Personally," Clint said, "I think it's as boring as hell, but people seem to be turning out for it."

"Boring?" Flatt looked hurt.

"I'm sorry," Clint said, "but you asked. I thought you'd want an honest answer."

"Yes, well," Flatt said, "I suppose it could be a little more exciting."

"I'm sure you'll think of a way," Clint said.

"Maybe," Flatt said, "if their dresses were a little more . . . revealing?"

"I'm sure Rita would help you with that," Clint said. "By the way, why did the MacLeod Brother's sister—Nancy, was it?—take her elimination so personally? She shouldn't have slapped you and called you a sonofabitch."

"I know," Flatt said. "I, uh, don't know what that was about." He hurriedly finished his beer. "Thanks for the drink, Clint."

"Another?"

"No," Flatt said, "I think I better get home to my wife."

"Ah, yes," Clint said, "you might have some explaining to do, eh?"

"I'm sure I do," Flatt said. "I'll see you in the morning."

"In the tent, right?"

"Yes," Flatt said, "in the tent."

"Good-night, then."

As Flatt went out the door, Clint ordered himself another beer.

***

Sitting at a table in the Gun Barrel, Mike Duffy watched as Clint Adams started drinking his second beer. He had told the mayor he wouldn't make a move against the Gunsmith, but that didn't mean he couldn't watch him.

"What's wrong with you, Mike?" his friend and partner, Gage Watkins, asked.

"Nothin'," Duffy said, "absolutely nothin'."

Somehow, that response didn't ring true with Watkins.

Chapter Thirty-Two

"That's the Gunsmith, ain't it?" Watkins asked. "I heard he was in town judgin' that Dance Hall contest."

"Yup, that's him," Duffy said, "and that's what he's doin'."

"How come we didn't go and see that?" Watkins asked. "We both like pretty girls."

"We got other things on our mind, Gage," Mike Duffy said.

"We do?"

"Yup."

"Like what?"

Duffy looked across the table at his friend, who was a lot better at doing what he was told than having things on his mind.

"I'll let you know when the time's right," he said.

"Well," Gage Watkins asked, "is the time right to have another beer? At least *that* way I get to have a close look at a pretty girl."

"Sure, Gage," Duffy said, "let's have us another coupla beers."

Watkins looked around, picked out a girl he thought he liked, and waved at her.

***

When he was in a saloon, and people knew who he was, Clint could always feel the eyes that were on him. Some were just curious glances that didn't last. Others were the kind of looks people gave to a dog with three legs, kind of interested, but after a few steps, not so much.

And then there was the kind he was feeling right now, like there was somebody in that saloon staring holes in him. He looked around, trying to find who had such an interest in him that it was making his skin itch.

He found two.

One was Amy, who would stare at him whenever she got the chance, which was when she wasn't busy serving drinks.

The other was a man who may not have wanted to be spotted but when he was, didn't look away. That was the worst kind, because that meant there was no indecisiveness in the man. He was confident enough to match stares when he was caught.

The man was sitting with another man, who was busy looking around the room, not paying any attention to Clint, at all. That was interesting, because it meant that the first man's interest was personal and was not being brought to the attention of his friend.

However, the man seemed content to watch, not antsy at all. He obviously wasn't itching to stand up and announce his intentions.

Clint decided to leave the man alone until he made up his mind about what he wanted to do. However, that didn't mean he was going to ignore him. Just keep an eye out.

He turned back and leaned on the bar.

***

Mike Duffy knew that the Gunsmith had spotted him. That was okay. He had no intention of doing anything at the moment, so let the man wait and wonder. Let the question burrow its way under his skin and start to itch. The time would come, soon enough.

***

"Another one?" the bartender asked Clint.

"I'm thinking."

"On the house?"

"You wouldn't be trying to bribe me, would you?" Clint asked.

"Hell, no," the bartender said. "I couldn't care less who wins that stupid contest."

"Why not?"

"I don't own the place," the man said. "Amy wins and goes to Fort Worth, it ain't me who's gonna have to find a replacement. You want that beer?"

"Sure," Clint said. "never turn down a free beer, right?"

"You got that right."

He was working on the free one when Amy sidled up to him, again.

"Where's your friend?" she asked.

"Had to go home to his wife."

"You know," she said, "some of the girls have tried to get to your hotel room."

"Is that right?"

"You must have that desk clerk trained right."

"I think he's just doin' his job."

"I wouldn't know," she said. "I ain't tried."

"Why not?"

"If I wanted to bribe you with a free poke or suck," she said, "I'd just take you upstairs to my own room."

"But you don't want to, right?"

She shook her head.

"I wanna win on my own."

"That's good."

"Mostly it's them Silver Dollar girls, Milly, Lisa and Kitty, tryin' to sneak up there."

"Mmmm," he said, "they're pretty, those Silver Dollar girls."

"Kinda," Amy agreed.

"But I don't think they're as pretty as, say, your sister, Penny."

"I keep tellin' her that," Amy said. "I don't know why she don't think she's pretty enough to be a saloon girl."

"I don't know, either," Clint said. "She's a good waitress, though."

"She'd make more money here," Amy said. "And that'd even be without taking men upstairs."

"Is that what she thinks she'd have to do?"

"She don't think she's pretty enough for a man to wanna go upstairs with her," Amy complained.

"That's a shame."

"Hey!" she said, suddenly. "I know what you could do."

"What?"

"Take her to bed," Amy said. "Show her you want her. That'd make her feel better about herself."

"I couldn't do that, Amy."

"Why not?"

"For one thing, she's too young," Clint said.

"She's twenty-two, plenty old enough."

"Too young for me," Clint added. "But maybe I'll have breakfast at the café where she works and try to talk some sense into her."

"And maybe you can get her to come and watch me tomorrow?" Amy asked.

"I'll try," Clint promised. "See you in the morning."

"Good-night, judge," she said, smiling.

Chapter Thirty-Three

But he didn't have breakfast at Penny's café the next morning. When he came down to the lobby, he found Rita waiting for him.

"How did it go with Nancy last night?" he asked.

"I calmed her down by giving her a dress," Rita said. "But do you know what she told me?"

"What?"

"She had sex with Randall in order to win the competition," she said. "That's why she slapped him."

"Are you sure?"

"Well," Rita said, "as she put it, she gave him a suck—twice."

"That surprises me," Clint said. "I didn't think he was the type."

"And he's not even a judge," she said. "How could he fix the results? If we give him our picks, and he changes them, we'd know."

"You're right."

She frowned.

"Has that happened to you?"

"What?"

"Have any of the girls offered you, a, uh, suck?" she asked.

"No," he said. "The desk clerk told me some of them tried to get to my room, but he stopped them."

"They want to win that bad?"

"For a trip to Fort Worth, yes."

"But . . . it's not that far," she said. "I've been to Fort Worth. It's not like they're playing for a trip to New York, or Paris."

"Rita, I'm sure some of these girls haven't even been outside of this town."

"I suppose you're right," she said. "Are you going to breakfast?"

"That was the plan."

"Can I join you?"

"I was just going to invite you," he said. "Jamaican?"

"No," she said, "Loretta doesn't serve breakfast."

"Then I know just the place," he told her.

And they went to Penny's café, after all.

***

"The waitress looks familiar," Rita said, after they ordered.

"That's because she's Amy's sister."

"Amy?"

"The blonde from the Gun Barrel."

"Oh, that one!" Rita said. "Yes, I can see the resemblance."

Penny brought over their plates, refilled their coffee cups and said, "Just let me know if you want anything else."

"She likes you."

"What?"

"I can tell," Rita said. "The way she looks at you and talks to you."

"Maybe you just think that because of what Nancy told you," Clint said. "It's affected your thinking."

"No, no," she said, "I know young girls. I can see the look in her eyes. She's infatuated."

"Well," Clint said, "she's very young, and besides, I have my hands full, right now."

"With me?" she asked, looking amused.

"I have all these girls in the contest," Clint said. "I don't need anymore."

"So not with me?"

"Oh, with you, too," he said. "Now eat your breakfast."

Chapter Thirty-Four

After breakfast they headed for the tent. Neither of them was looking forward to it.

"Somehow I didn't think this would be such a bore," Rita said.

"The only thing that saves it for me is sitting next to you," Clint said.

"Flatterer!"

Randall Flatt came running over to them, looking harried.

"We have some time," he said to Rita. "Can you help me?"

"With what?"

"I'll tell you on the way!"

Rita looked at Clint, shrugged, and said, "All right," and went with Flatt.

The mayor came in at that point and sat one seat away from Clint, leaving Rita's chair empty.

"Where's our lady friend?" he asked.

"She's here," Clint assured him. "Randall came and got her. He needed help with something."

"Probably some woman thing," the mayor said.

"I'm sure," Clint said.

Abruptly, the mayor moved over to sit next to Clint. The row of people behind them were quiet.

"How does it feel to be the center of attention?" he asked.

"I could ask you the same thing," Clint said. "Isn't that what being a politician is all about?"

"Well, yes, but with me it's the need for votes," the mayor said. "With you it's everyone around you waiting for you to kill somebody."

"I don't think it's that bad," Clint said. "And, anyway, if you knew I'd be the center of attention, why ask me to judge and take attention away from the competition?"

"You know?" Hunter said. "That's what I asked Randall when he told me he was going to ask you to judge."

"And?"

"He thought you'd attract more attention to the event than you'd take away from it." The mayor looked around at the interior of the tent. "I hate to say it, but he may have been right."

"Glad to help."

The mayor ended the conversation by moving back to his own seat. He started to talk to the people on his right, probably drumming up votes for the next election.

After a short while people in the audience began to get antsy, and Clint wondered what the problem could be that required Rita's help? He remembered Randall Flatt saying something about the girls perhaps showing more skin. Maybe that was it.

Suddenly, she reappeared and sat down, with a put-upon expression on her face.

"What's going on?"

"Randall wanted me to help with the dresses," she said. "He wants the girls to show more skin."

"And?"

"There's not enough time for that now," she said. "The girls are coming to my store later, so we can work on it. I'll probably be at it all day! He wants them to wear the new dresses tonight."

"New dresses?"

"Well, no," she said, "just the old ones."

"How do the girls feel about it?"

"Are you kidding?" she asked. "Half of them offered to walk out here naked!"

"At least that'd really get this thing some attention," Clint said.

"Randall's going ahead with his scheduled event, and later we'll work on the dresses for tonight, when we eliminate four more girls."

At that point Flatt came out on stage and addressed the audience.

"Ladies and gentlemen," he said, "here are our remaining eight contestants for Miss Dance Hall!"

***

Mike Duffy stood across the street from the Bank of Redwind, watching the foot traffic, as it thinned out. There were two other banks in town, and across the street from them were men who worked for Duffy. Neither could believe they were going to rob a bank on their own, but there they were waiting. Duffy had given them a time to move, explaining that it would be just as the Miss Dance Hall girls were coming out on stage again.

Duffy had chosen these two men carefully. Not especially smart boys, but they usually did what they were told. When he gave them specific instructions, they usually followed them to the letter.

With five minutes to go all three men pulled their bandanas up to cover the bottom of their faces. Just as Duffy had told them, the street was now empty. The men simply stepped into the street, crossed over to the bank, drew their guns, and walked in.

Chapter Thirty-Five

The girls droned on, answering inane questions put to them by Randall Flatt. Not for the first time Clint realized that Flatt was not the man to run a competition like this. The mayor was the smart one, so there had to be a reason he would have chosen Flatt for this task. Clint looked over at the politician's profile. He appeared more like a mortician than a mayor—a mortician with a smile on his face. What could the man be seeing that was making him so happy?

Or what could he be thinking?

He nudged Rita.

"Yes?"

"Talk to the mayor."

"About what?" she asked.

"Anything," he said. "He just looks too happy with himself. Make conversation, flatter him, talk about the girls, see what you can find out."

"Okay."

She leaned the other way and started a conversation with him, keeping her voice low.

Clint noticed something else. Flatt was running this show all by himself, didn't have any help. Maybe that's why he was so anxious to recruit Rita as more than just a judge.

The girls began to show their other talents. Some sang, some danced, some even recited poetry. Once again it went on for hours.

Finally, Flatt stood center stage and announced that the eliminations would be announced at 7 p.m. People started filing out.

The mayor and Rita stood up, exchanged a few more words, and then he turned to leave.

"See you later, Adams," he called out.

"Sure, Mr. Mayor."

As he left Rita turned to Clint.

"He's funny," she said.

"Funny? How?"

"He didn't even want to talk about this competition," she said.

"What did he want to talk about?"

"His career," she said. "He's apparently got big plans to run for higher offices."

"That's not a surprise," he said, "but that kind of thing takes a war chest."

"A what?"

"Money."

"You think he's making money from this contest?" she asked.

"Either from it," Clint said, "or because of it."

"What do you mean?"

"I don't know, Rita," Clint said. "I just have to think about it. Supper?"

"I've got to spend the next two hours at my store with the girls," she said. "But I'll be back here at seven. How about a late meal after?"

Clint wasn't that hungry, so he agreed to wait and eat with her after the eliminations.

***

Clint spent the two hours in his room, reading and making his list of eliminations, which would probably change once he saw the girls in their new dresses. When he came out there was a murmur going through the lobby, and he was aware of something on the street.

"What's going on?" he asked the middle-aged desk clerk.

"Ain't you heard?" the man asked. "Bank robbery."

"What?"

"Yeah," the clerk said, "while everybody was in that tent today lookin' at pretty girls, the banks were robbed."

"Banks?" Clint asked. "How many?"

"All three," the clerk said.

"They know who did it?"

"The words goin' around," the clerk said. "Nobody knows who done it, but it was three different men."

"How do they know that?"

"The way they figure it, they were all robbed at the same time."

If that was the case, then it couldn't be the same man who robbed all three.

Clint left the lobby and headed for the tent.

***

Word had gotten around, all right, but the tent was still half full of people waiting to hear about the eliminations.

"Did you hear?" Rita asked him.

"I heard," Clint said. "Where's Randall?"

"He's really upset. He's over there, talking to the mayor."

Clint walked over to the two men. As he approached, they stopped talking and turned to him.

"What's the word, Mayor?" Clint said.

"All three banks were robbed at the same time, the mayor said, "while most of the town was in here."

"That ain't my fault!" Flatt blurted.

"Who says it was, Randall?" Clint asked.

"Nobody, but the way they're looking at me—"

"Relax, Randall," the mayor said. "The sheriff's working on it."

"The sheriff!" Flatt said. "He's useless."

"What's he doing about it?" Clint asked.

"Well, first he's trying to find his two deputies," the mayor said. "apparently, they went fishing."

"So most of the town was in here and the deputies were fishing," Clint said. "What about the sheriff, himself?"

"In his office," Mayor Hunter said.

"So who saw the robberies?"

"The people in the banks," the mayor said. "The tellers and the managers."

"What'd they see?"

"A man with a mask covering the lower part of his face, and a gun in his hand."

"And that's it?"

"That's it."

"So they won't be able to identify them?"

"Not a chance," the mayor said.

"So why are you here?" Clint asked. "Looks like half of the crowd lost interest in this contest."

"They had their money in the banks," Flatt said. "So did I, but I've got to keep this thing going."

"I agree," the mayor said. "This may be all this town has going for it, right now."

Flatt went to see about the girls, while the mayor and Clint went to sit with Rita.

Chapter Thirty-Six

"Why would somebody do such a thing?" Rita asked.

"Because they could," Clint said. "Everybody's attention was elsewhere, so all they had to do was come up with the idea, get two other men to help him, and do it. Seems like it was timed perfectly.

The mayor leaned across Rita, who wasn't thrilled about it.

"Adams, I don't suppose you'd take a job as a special deputy and look into the robberies, would you?"

"Not me, Mr. Mayor," Clint said. "You've got a sheriff. I didn't come here looking for trouble."

"Randall's right, though," the mayor said. "Our sheriff isn't worth much."

"But he's what you've got," Clint said, "so you're stuck with him."

"I suppose you're right, the mayor said, and leaned back into his chair.

"What happened with the dresses?" Clint asked Rita.

"You'll see," she said. "I did the best I could with the time I had."

And he did see—a lot!

When the girls came out they were pretty much wearing the same dresses, but now they were showing more skin. There were a lot of rounded shoulders and exposed upper breasts. Some of them even exposed a lot of leg.

The men in the tent showed their appreciation by whistling and calling out bawdy remarks.

"Good job," Clint said to Rita.

"Thanks." She really didn't mean it.

"No, no," the mayor said, "you've done a fine job, Rita, a fine job. Listen to these people."

Rita looked around.

"They sound like a crowd in a cheap saloon."

"These *are* saloon girls," Clint pointed out.

"Then why is this contest called Miss Dance Hall?" she asked.

"That was my doing," the mayor said. "It just sounds more respectable."

"What's the Fort Worth contest called?" Clint asked.

"Miss Texas," he said.

The girls were prancing around stage, now, trying to show even more skin to the crowd. As judges, of course, the three of them had to look as well.

Randall Flatt was standing off to the side, looking worried. Clint wondered why. There might have been less people in the tent, but all the tickets he had for sale had been sold. The competition was making its money— hopefully he hadn't put any of it in the bank, yet.

Flatt decided to take a chance and had the girls file off stage and around the room. There were women in the audience, who looked closely at the dresses, but the men ogled the girls, some even grabbed at them. Experienced with these kinds of grasping hands, the girls had no trouble eluding them. Eventually, they made their way back up onto the stage and once more around before filing off.

"Ladies and gents, the judges will now prepare their eliminations and we'll get right to it," Flatt explained, "so just be patient."

Flatt came down off the stage and said to the judges, "Go ahead and make your decision now."

"Without thinking it over?" Rita asked.

"I'm afraid if we let these people leave they may not come back," Flatt said. "Come on, you must have your favorites."

"All right, Randall," the mayor said, "just give us a chance to compare notes."

"Okay," Flatt said. "Let's do it in fifteen minutes, huh?"

"We'll give it our best try," the mayor assured him.

Chapter Thirty-Seven

Clint, Rita and the mayor compared notes, and came up with four names. Two girls—Kitty and Milly—from the Silver Dollar made the final four, along with Amy from the Gun Barrel and a girl named Hermione from a little saloon called The Red Rose, which Clint still had never seen in town.

"Where's the Red Rose?" he asked Rita.

"I have no idea, but she's stunning," Rita said. "I think she has the most perfect body I've ever worked with in my store."

Clint cast his eyes on the 4 girls now standing in the center of the stage. Amy was a slender blonde with a pretty face and an attitude that struck a chord with him. Kitty was a chubby blonde with amazingly pale skin and a baby face that stood out in stark contrast to her curvy body. Milly was a tall, stately redhead. And Hermione was a well-built brunette who was a bit older than the other 3, seemed more confident and assured in her movements and—according to Rita—had a perfect body.

"I know what you're doing," Rita said

"What am I doing?"

"You're imagining Hermione naked in bed," Rita said. "That's not what I mean by a 'perfect body,'" she explained. "I mean for dresses. She seemed to be the perfect height and have the perfect waist and bust to fit any dress."

"Oh."

"If she doesn't win and go to Fort Worth, I might hire her to work in my store. If I can show my dresses on a perfect body, I think I could sell more."

"Well," Clint said, "good luck to you both, then."

"Ladies and gents," Randall Flatt said, "be back here tomorrow morning at nine for the last of our events, and tomorrow night we'll announce the winner of Miss Dance Hall."

People got up and filed out. Some of the men went up to the stage to try to talk to the girls but had no luck. The ladies filed off the stage and out of the tent. If Amy was any example, they were all going back to work.

The mayor had left, as well, so it was only Clint, Rita and Randall Flatt in the tent. Flatt was sitting on the edge of the stage with his head down. Clint and Rita approached him.

"It can't be that bad," Rita said. "The audience seemed to love the new dresses."

"Oh, they did," Flatt assured her. "At least, the men did. I'm thinking about the bank robberies."

"Did you have your store account in one of them?" Clint asked, already knowing the answer. If you were running a business in this town, of course you had an account in one of the banks.

"Store and personal," Flatt said. "I know I'm going to get an earful when I get home."

"Your wife can't blame you for the banks being robbed," Rita said.

"You're not married, Rita," he said. "She's going to have to blame somebody. She'll say my stupid contest took everyone's attention away from the banks. And she's probably right."

"Or," Clint said, "somebody simply took advantage of the situation."

"Still my fault," he said, shaking his head. He slipped off the edge of the stage and stood up. "I guess I better get it over with."

The three of them walked out of the tent together.

"Cheer up, Randall," Clint said, slapping him on the back. "The bank robbers could get caught."

"Not with Sheriff Ritch on the job," Flatt said. He waved at the two of them and headed home.

"If he's that unhappy being married to his wife, then why stay?" Rita asked.

"To some people there's no question of leaving a marriage," Clint told her.

"No matter what the situation is?"

Clint shrugged.

"I suppose I'm fortunate that I've turned down every proposal of marriage I've ever had," she said.

"I've got a proposal for you," he said, "one I don't think you'll turn down."

***

Mike Duffy was waiting for Mayor Hunter when he got to his office.

"Lowry let you in?" Hunter asked, seating himself behind his desk.

"He did."

"Did it all go off as planned?"

"So far," Duffy said.

"What's that mean?"

"It means I still have to pick up the money from the other two," Duffy told him.

"Might that be a problem?" the mayor asked.

"There's always a chance."

"You mean those two might just light out with the money?" Hunter asked.

"It's possible."

"I thought you said they could be trusted."

"Mayor," Duffy said, "they robbed a bank. How trustworthy could they be?"

Chapter Thirty-Eight

Rita rolled onto her back and stared at the ceiling while trying to catch her breath. Her full breasts, topped by large, light brown nipples, heaved with the effort.

"You're quite right, Clint," she gasped. "That was a proposal I would've been foolish not to accept."

Clint settled down onto his back next to her, trying to catch his breath, as well.

"I wonder how Randall would feel if I wrote your name down as my winner," Clint said.

"Me?" she said. "But I'm not a saloon girl."

"Maybe not, but right now, you're my choice for Miss Texas."

"That's sweet," she said, "but right now I'm not so glad I agreed to do this."

"I can't say I blame you," Clint said. "I didn't expect to be around during a bank robbery."

"They're probably going to ask for your help," she observed.

"No," he said, "no, no, I'm not chasing bank robbers. I came here to do something different."

She propped herself up on her elbow and reached for his semi-hard cock.

"Is this different?"

"It's always different," he assured her.

"Really?" she asked. "Have you been with many women?" She stroked him.

"Yes, many."

"Hmm. Okay, then." She slid down so that her face was in his lap. "Tell me if this is different."

He settled back while she took him into her hot mouth. . .

***

Mike Duffy entered The Red Rose Saloon, saw the girl Hermione serving drinks to his two bank robbery partners.

These were not men he usually worked with. He had decided that his regular crew was untrustworthy. He decided to recruit two new men, who didn't know him as well. He needed them to be afraid of him.

"Beer," he said to Hermione, as he sat.

"Comin' up."

Trevor Deets and Mitch Robin looked across the table at him. They were both in their 30s and had also never worked together before.

"I'm glad to find you fellas here," Duffy said.

"Did you think we'd light out with the bank money?" Deets asked.

"I thought it was a possibility."

"But if we did that you'd . . . kill us," Robin said.

"Right."

"So here we are," Deets said.

They paused while Hermione set down Duffy's beer.

"Also," Duffy said, "if you did leave you wouldn't be in line for the big pay day in Fort Worth."

"Yeah," Deets said, "tell us about that one."

"Not yet," Duffy said. "It's still in the future. But for now, I need the money. Where is it?"

"Not far from here," Deets said.

"Mine's in my room, at the boarding house," Mitch Robin said.

Duffy stared at him.

"Don't worry, the door's locked," Robin said.

"Okay, look," Duffy said, "I have to pick up the money from both of you."

"Do we get paid?"

"Yes," Duffy said, "and then you leave town, and tell me where you end up. I'll get in touch when we're ready for Fort Worth."

"What about a posse?" Deets asked.

"What about it?" Duffy asked.

"Is there gonna be one?"

"I doubt it," Duffy said. "Not with this sheriff."

"But the Gunsmith is in town," Robin said. "What about him?"

"He's a little busy with something else," Duffy said. "And I'll be taking care of him later."

"When?" Deets asked.

"When I get the word."

"I'd like to see that," Robin said.

"Well, you won't," Duffy said. "You're both leaving and I'll see you in Fort Worth. Right?"

"Right," Deets said, and Robin nodded.

"Finish your drinks and we'll go and collect the money," Duffy said.

***

"So?" Rita said.

"So what?" Clint asked.

Once again they were lying side-by-side, only this time he was more out of breath than she was, owing to the massive eruption he had directed into her hot, insistent mouth.

"Was it different?"

"Unique," he said. "No other woman is like you."

She slapped him on the stomach and said, "Liar!" laughing. "Now you better go so we can both get some sleep."

Chapter Thirty-Nine

Clint had breakfast alone the next morning, so he could do some thinking. For that reason, too, he did not go to the café where Penny worked. He wanted to eat someplace where no one would talk to him.

It was possible that the entire Miss Dance Hall competition was put on to distract all attention away from the banks so they could be robbed. But who would devise such a plan? Certainly not Randall Flatt. That would be too obvious. And to Clint he did not seem the type.

So then who?

The man who appointed Flatt to run the competition was the mayor. But why would the mayor of a town have his own banks robbed? It would reflect badly on the sheriff of the town, and the town itself. But what if he didn't care, because he had higher aspirations? And if that was the case, who would he get to rob the banks for him?

And if the mayor was behind the bank robberies, would his assistant, Lowry, know anything about it? Perhaps the only way to find that out was to ask him.

***

After breakfast Clint walked over to City Hall. He still had an hour before he had to report to the tent. He went inside and up to the mayor's office. As he entered, he saw Edward Lowry seated at his desk outside the mayor's office. He looked up as Clint approached.

"The mayor's not here," Lowry said. "I think he was going directly to the tent."

"I was looking for you, Mr. Lowry."

"Me? But why?"

"I was curious about the bank robberies."

"What about them?"

"Has there been any luck identifying the robbers?" Clint asked.

"Huh? Luck? No, nothing that I know of," Lowry said.

"The witnesses don't have anything helpful to say?" Clint asked.

"Witnesses."

"Well, there were witnesses, weren't there?"

"I'm sure the sheriff—"

"I haven't heard good things about Sheriff Ritch."

"That doesn't matter," Lowry said. "For now he's the sheriff."

"So what's he doing?"

"Damned if I know," Lowry said. "I'm just the mayor's assistant. You'll have to talk to him about that."

"Where were you when the banks were being robbed?" Clint asked.

"I was—" Lowry stopped short. "Why are you asking me that?"

"I'm curious," Clint said. "I know the mayor was in the tent with me during the competition. But where were you?"

"Not that it's any of your business," Lowry said, "but I was right here, working."

"And the robberies were committed without a shot being fired?"

"Apparently so."

"They must have been very well planned."

"If you're so concerned," Lowry said, "why don't you go and talk to the sheriff?"

"You know what?" Clint said, "that's a good idea."

Clint left City Hall, unconvinced that Lowry wasn't somehow involved with at least planning the robberies.

***

As he entered the sheriff's office a man looked up at him from the desk. He was at least 60 and looked as if he was permanently ensconced in his chair. A man of action would not settle into his chair as comfortably.

"Clint Adams, isn't it?" he asked.

"Are you Sheriff Ritch?" Clint asked.

"That's me."

"I'm Adams."

"Have a seat, then," Ritch said. "Tell me what I can do for you."

"I'm curious about the bank robberies yesterday."

"So am I," Ritch said. "Seems to me it was a well-planned strike."

"What have you been doing about it?" Clint asked.

"First off I'm still tryin' to find my deputies," Ritch said.

"Is that what you were doing when I came in?"

Ritch frowned.

"Why do I have to explain myself to you?" he asked.

"You don't," Clint said. "I was just . . . curious."

The sheriff looked at the clock on his wall.

"And don't you have to be somewhere?"

"I was just thinking about who could've planned the robberies to coincide with the Miss Dance Hall competition," Clint explained.

"Co-in-what?"

"Planned to happen at the same time."

"Oh," the older man said. "Well, I'll have my deputies look into it as soon as they get back."

Clint stood up, realizing that what he had heard about the sheriff was right.

"Good luck," Clint said, and headed for the tent.

Chapter Forty

Randall Flatt had the girls strut around the stage in their new dresses, while Clint, Rita and the mayor made up their minds about who would win Miss Dance Hall and go to Fort Worth to represent Redwind, Texas.

"It's got to be Hermione," the mayor insisted.

"Why her?" Rita asked.

"She's older," the mayor said. "She'll be able to handle Fort Worth better than these other, younger girls."

Rita turned her head.

"Clint?" she asked.

"He might be right, Rita," Clint said. "Besides, you almost convinced me with that talk about her having the perfect body."

"I suppose . . ."

They discussed it further, decided on their winner with Amy as the runner-up.

"She has a great attitude," Rita said. "If the winner can't go to Fort Worth, then Amy should go."

Clint and the mayor agreed, and they handed their decision up to Randall Flatt, on stage.

"Ladies and gentlemen, we have our judge's decision," Flatt announced.

The tent was about three-quarters filled, with some of the people having returned from the day before.

"The winner of Miss Dance Hall, and the contestant going on to Fort Worth is . . . Hermione!"

Hermione stepped forward, acting surprised while the audience applauded. Amy hugged her, but the other girls stormed off. That worked out, because Flatt then announced that Amy had come in second.

"Thank you to our judges," Flatt said, "and thank you all for coming."

The people stood up and began to file out.

"Fine job, you two," the mayor said, and rose to follow the crowd.

"I'm glad he thinks so," Rita said.

"I have a feeling he's happy about something else," Clint said.

"Like what?" she asked.

"Why don't we go someplace private and I'll tell you," he said.

"If we go someplace private," she asked, "are we going to talk?"

"Eventually," he said.

***

Before going off on their own they stopped to talk with Randall Flatt.

"So when does Hermione leave for Fort Worth, Randall?" Clint asked.

"The end of the month," Flatt said.

"Is Redwind footing the bill to get her there?" Clint asked. "Or the Red Rose?"

"That saloon? Not a chance."

"So the town?"

"They were going to," Flatt said, "but now that the banks got robbed, I don't know if even the town can afford it."

"So what about the mayor?"

"I'll bet he has the money in his house to pay for it," Flatt said. "The question is, will he? He's quite a miser."

"Saving for his war chest?" Rita asked.

Flatt looked at her, surprised.

"That's right. How'd you figure that out?"

She looked at Clint.

"I had some help from a friend," she said.

"I guess we'll just have to wait and see if she gets to Fort Worth," Flatt said, shaking his head. "This sure didn't go the way I thought it would."

As Flatt walked away, Clint said, "It went the way somebody thought it would."

"There you go again," Rita said. "What are you talking about?"

"Let's go and get some coffee and I'll tell you."

***

They went to the café where Penny worked, and she brought them the coffee.

"I heard Amy came in second," she said. "I'm real proud of her."

"How does she feel about it?" Rita asked.

"Oh, she'll be okay," Penny said. "Hermione may work in a dump, but she's a beautiful woman. Anybody can see that. Lemme know if you want anything else, Clint."

"I will, kid," Clint said. "Thanks."

"She's not a kid," Rita told him. "And she's got a big yen for you."

"I told you before," he reminded her. "I've got my hands full."

"The competition is over," she said.

"We're not."

Chapter Forty-One

"You're kidding!" Rita said, while they drank their coffee. "You think the mayor had his own town banks robbed?"

"It's a possibility."

"But why?"

"The whole war chest matter," Clint said. "he has to put together a lot of money for a serious run for Congress, the Senate, or the Governor's Mansion."

"But how could he do any of that if he's a crook?"

"Are you kidding?" Clint asked. "That's a perfect recommendation for a politician."

"I suppose," she said, grudgingly, "but they're not all crooked."

"Most of them are," Clint said, "believe me. I've been in Washington D.C. enough times to know."

"So the town suffers," she said.

"And he'll pretend to suffer," Clint said.

"Isn't he taking a big chance?"

"Not when this town's got Sheriff Ritch looking out for it," he pointed out.

"Why do you care?" she asked. "You came here to judge a contest, and it's over. Your job is done. You can just leave this all behind."

"And that's what I should do."

"But you won't?" she asked, looking amused.

"Probably not," Clint said. "I don't always know what's best for me."

"So are you going after the bank robbers?" she asked. "With a posse?"

"No."

"Why not?"

"Well, for one thing I wouldn't know which members of the posse were also the bank robbers."

"So you don't think they're gone?"

"If I'm right about the mayor being involved," he said, "or even Lowry, then no, I don't think they're gone. I think they're here, somewhere. And so's the money."

"So then you're going to find the money?"

"Maybe," he said. "I just don't like the idea of it going into the mayor's war chest."

"Ah, you don't like the mayor."

"I don't like politicians," Clint said. "And if my coming here to judge the contest helped him rob the banks, then yes, I want to find the money and get it away from him."

"But first, don't you have to be sure he did it?" she asked.

"Yes, I do."

"And how are you going to do that?"

"The easiest way," he said. "I'm going to ask him."

***

Clint paid the check and told Rita he'd see her later. As he walked out the door, Penny came running after him.

"Oh, Mr. Adams," she said. "I'm glad I caught you."

"It's Clint, remember?"

"Yes, of course," she said, "Clint. Uh, how did Amy take it when she, uh, didn't win?"

"You haven't talked to her?"

"Um, no, I haven't."

"She took it quite well, like you said she would," he told her. "After all, she came in second. If Hermione can't go to Fort Worth, then Amy would get to go."

"I see."

"And to tell you the truth," he added, "Hermione may not be able to afford the trip. So if the Gun Barrel gets behind Amy, she may end up going."

"That's very interestin'," she said.

"You should talk to her," he added. "Look, I have to go do a few things."

"Of course," she said. "Thanks." And went back inside.

***

Edward Lowry looked up from his desk again as Clint entered.

"Now what?" he asked.

"I want to see the mayor."

Lowry looked relieved.

"He's in his office," he said, jerking his thumb. "Go ahead in."

"Don't you want to announce me first?"

"No."

Clint went to the door to the mayor's office and walked right in.

"Mr. Adams," the mayor said, from behind his desk. "Isn't Edward out there?"

"He is," Clint said. "He told me to come right in."

"Well," Hunter said, "I see he and I are going to have to have a talk about his job. What can I do for you?"

"You can answer a question for me."

"Of course," the man said, "if I can."

"Were you behind the bank robberies?" Clint asked.

Chapter Forty-Two

"What the hell—"

"Hold on," Clint said. "I'm not done. The fact that those robberies took place while most of the town's attention was on the Miss Dance Hall contest is too much of a coincidence, don't you think?"

"No," the mayor said. "I think somebody saw an opportunity to take advantage of the fact. Have you asked Randall Flatt?"

"Not him. You're the one, trying to fill up your war chest."

Mayor Hunter stared at Clint.

"Aren't you done here?" he asked. "The competition is over. Isn't it time for you to leave town?"

"You'd think so, wouldn't you," Clint asked. "But I'm not finished, yet."

"I think you are," the mayor said. "You know your way out."

Clint turned and walked out. He stopped and leaned on Lowry's desk.

"If you were in on this, I'll be taking care of you, too," he said.

"What?"

"Think about it and let me know what you decide."

He left before Lowry could close his mouth.

***

"Back so soon?" Sheriff Ritch asked. He looked as if he had not moved since Clint left.

"I spoke with the mayor, and with Lowry," Clint said. "If the mayor wanted to have the banks robbed, who would he use?"

"What?"

"You heard me."

"Look, Adams, this is my job—"

"Which you're not doing," Clint said. "And I'm not asking you to. I'm just asking you a simple question. Who in this town would rob the banks for the mayor?"

"I can't—"

"Sheriff," Clint said, "I'm not leaving Redwind until I find that money and put the mayor in one of your cells. Now you can either answer my questions, or I'll put you in the cell next to him."

Sheriff Ritch stared at Clint a few moments, then said, "Have a seat. Let me think a minute."

***

The sheriff gave Clint a few names, but he didn't feel he had the time to check them all out. The mayor might already be planning to move the money. So he decided to ask somebody else for help.

When he got to the Gun Barrel it had just opened for the day. There was only a couple of customers, and neither one was standing at the bar. The bartender looked at him as he approached.

"Beer?"

"Yes, thanks."

When he set the beer down Clint asked, "Gardner, right?"

"That's right," the man said. "Mark."

"Mark, I'm Clint," Clint said, "and I need your help."

Gardner leaned his elbows on the bar.

"With what?"

"Some names."

"Of who?"

"Bank robbers."

Gardner looked surprised.

"Well, I mean, potential bank robbers," Clint corrected.

"Are you tryin' to find who robbed our banks?"

"I am."

"Well then, I'm in. I'll help any way I can."

"I think I know who was behind it," Clint said, "but not who actually pulled the jobs."

"Who are we talkin' about?"

"I'll tell you later," Clint said. "Right now I've got four names, and I need you to tell me what you know about them."

"Okay, shoot."

"Gage Watkins, Hal Elder, Jeff Stewart and Mike Duffy," Clint said. "Any of them strike you as the type who would pull those jobs, if they were being paid to?"

"Paid to," Gardner said. "That's the key. A couple of those boys would do anythin' if they were paid enough."

"Which ones?"

"Duffy and Watkins," Gardner said. "They're partners. In fact . . . you saw 'em . . ."

"I did? When?"

"You was in here the other night and I saw Duffy watchin' you."

"I noticed a man watching me, too. That was Mike Duffy?"

"Yeah," Gardner said. "I didn't think nothin' of it at the time, just thought he was thinkin' about tryin' you. He's pretty good with a gun."

"Have you seen him around since then?"

"As a matter of fact, no," he said. "But I have seen Watkins. He was in here lookin' for Duffy. Said he hadn't seen him for a while."

"If Duffy did it, wouldn't he use Watkins?"

"You'd think so, but Gage kept sayin' he couldn't find 'im. Said he was afraid Duffy had found himself a job without him."

Clint smiled.

"I knew I came to the right place."

Chapter Forty-Three

Clint could have waited for Gage Watkins to come to the Gun Barrel later that evening, but he didn't want to give the mayor that much time. So Gardner gave him an idea of where Watkins might be at that time of the day.

Clint spent the afternoon looking for Watkins, hoping that the mayor's massive ego would keep him from moving too quickly to hide the money.

Gardner gave Clint 4 options, and 3 of them were saloons. The 4th was the Redwind brothel, and that was the last place Clint checked.

"Who?" the girl at the door asked. She was a young brunette wearing a nightgown which wasn't designed to attract men. He assumed she had just awakened to face the day.

"Watkins, Gage Watkins," Clint said. "Is he in there, with one of the girls?"

"He might be," she said. "Men don't usually come here and use their real names."

"Well," he said, "there's got to be one girl in there who knows him?"

"There probably is," she said. "Come on in."

He walked past her as she closed the door.

"We're not really open right now, but there are a couple of men upstairs."

"One of them may be a bank robber," Clint said. "I'll have to go up and find out."

"I'll have to check with Miss Lila," the girl said. "She runs the place. Are you the law?"

"No."

"Okay, then. Wait here and I'll go ask—"

"You go ask and I'll go upstairs and check," he said. "That way we're both being productive."

"Huh?"

"I'll see you when I come down."

He ran up the stairs before she could object.

With the first door he opened he surprised a redhead who was getting dressed. She was bent over, pulling on her underwear, naked, pendulous breasts swinging as she did so.

"Hey!" she objected.

"Sorry."

The second door revealed a sleeping brunette, full-bodied and naked, who didn't even move. He stared at her big ass for a few moments, then withdrew and closed the door.

The third door revealed a bed with two sleeping girls cuddled together. One opened her eyes, smiled at him and waved for him to join them.

"Maybe next time," he said, and closed the door.

The fourth door revealed a man on top of a woman, plowing away at her, both of them grunting and groaning. All he could see of the woman was long, skinny legs. He saw too much of the man.

"Gage Watkins?" he asked.

"Next door!" the man roared.

"Thanks," Clint said. "Carry on."

He went to the next room and opened the door. A man was lying on his back, his hands behind his head, while a girl was busy down between his legs.

"Sorry to interrupt," Clint said.

The girl stopped what she was doing, turned and looked at him.

"Gage Watkins?" Clint asked.

"Next room," the man said. "You missed it."

"He said this room," Clint replied.

"He's tellin' the truth, Mister," the girl said. "This ain't Gage. Can I go back to work?"

"Go ahead."

He slammed the door, ran to the previous room. As he opened the door the man was hopping around, trying to get his second leg into his trousers. The girl on the bed was watching.

"Watkins!" Clint said.

The man stopped hopping, looked over at his gunbelt, hanging on a chair.

"Don't try it," Clint said.

The girl on the bed covered her head with both arms.

"Whataya want?" Watkins asked. He was a grim looking man in his 30s.

"Just to talk," Clint said.

"About what?"

"Duffy."

The man straightened and seemed to relax.

"Why didn't you say so?" He looked at the girl. "You can go, Clara."

The girl sprang off the bed and ran from the room, moving quickly on those long, skinny legs.

Watkins sat on the bed, his trousers now pulled up but not buttoned, bare-chested and bare-foot.

"What's your interest in that sonofabitch?" he asked.

"Why's he a sonofabitch?"

"I know he's got a job he didn't include me in," Watkins said. "We're supposed to be partners."

"The bank robberies?"

Watkins' eyes widened.

"He did that?"

"I'm asking you," Clint said. "Would he?"

"Now that I think of it," Watkins said, "it was done so easily, I can see that it might have been him."

"On his own, or would he have been hired to do it?"

Watkins thought a moment.

"Duffy is always a man ready to do a job," Watkins said. "If you think he robbed those banks, then he was hired to do it."

"And who would he get to do it with him? Men he could trust?"

"No," Watkins said, "if he was gonna do that he woulda used me. No, he'd use men who don't know him real well, men he could scare."

"Where can I find Duffy, Watkins?"

"Look," Watkins said, "I may be mad at him, but that don't mean I'm gonna help you catch him."

"Then if I can't catch him," Clint said, "I'll catch you."

"I told you, I didn't have nothin' to do with it," Watkins said.

"But you also told me you're his partner."

"I'm supposed to be his partner," the man said, "but if he pulled this . . . you know what, I *will* tell you where to find him. But I'll also tell you to watch your ass."

"I always do . . ."

Chapter Forty-Four

Gage Watkins told Clint that Mike Duffy had a house outside of town. He said it was a rundown place off by itself, so he better watch himself if he was going out there.

It was north of town, and Clint approached on foot. It was quiet, and his instincts told him there was nobody inside. The house was a one-story, dilapidated wooden structure that looked to only be one or two rooms. He peered in a window, saw no one, then tried the front door and found it unlocked. When he entered he saw a cot, a table, a couple of chairs, and a pot-bellied stove in the center of it all. As old as it looked, there was not that layer of dust that aged structures usually have, and the cot looked as if it had been recently slept on. So if Watkins was right, it was Duffy who was living there—virtually hiding out.

Clint opened the stove, found cold ashes. He had been hoping to also find some money hidden inside, but that would have been too easy. But if this was Duffy's hideout, and he *was* the bank robber, then the money might be hidden somewhere nearby.

Clint saw a shovel in a corner, so he grabbed it, went outside and started searching. Behind the house he found an empty hole by a tree. It meant that the money had been there, but had been dug up. Was Duffy turning the money over to the mayor? If so, certainly not in broad daylight.

From the look of the pile of dirt next to the hole, it had been dug up recently—maybe even since Clint had gone to see the mayor.

Maybe going to see him had been a mistake.

But maybe the thing to do was go and see him again.

***

Lowry entered the Red Rose, saw Mike Duffy sitting alone at a table.

"What's this about?" Duffy asked. "Where's the mayor?"

"He can't come," Lowry said, sitting. "He doesn't want the two of you to be seen together."

"Why not?"

"The Gunsmith," Lowry said, looking at the canvas bag that was sitting at Duffy's feet. "Is that . . . all the money?"

"It is," Duffy said. "I thought Hunter was coming here to get it."

"He can't," Lowry said. "The Gunsmith went to see him. He suspects that the mayor was behind the bank robberies."

"So does he want me to give you the money?"

"Hell, no!" Lowry said. "I don't want it."

"Good, because I ain't about to do that," Duffy said. "So what's the plan?"

"The mayor wants you to do two things."

"What?"

"One, bring the money to his house tonight after dark," Lowry said.

"And second?"

"Kill the Gunsmith."

Duffy grinned.

"I been looking forward to that," he said. "I can do that first—"

"No," Lowry said, "the mayor was very precise about this. First bring him the money, then kill the Gunsmith."

"But why wait?" Duffy asked. "I can get it done to-day."

Lowry's eyes flicked around the room.

"What are you not telling me?" Duffy asked.

"The mayor's just worried that . . ."

"That what?"

"Well . . . if you go against the Gunsmith too soon, he might kill you, and then . . ."

" . . . and then the mayor won't know where the money is."

"That's right," Lowry said, "that is, unless you tell me now where you'll hide it."

Duffy laughed.

"Tell Hizzoner I'll see him tonight at his house."

Chapter Forty-Five

When Clint entered, Lowry wasn't at his desk. That suited him. He didn't like the little man. He went into the mayor's office.

"Again?" Hunter asked, looking up from his desk. "I'm going to have to fire Edward."

"He's not there," Clint said. "I just want to tell you I'll be watching every way in and out of this town, in case your boys try to sneak that money out."

"We still talking about bank robbery proceeds?" the mayor asked.

"Yep."

"And by my boys you mean the actual bank robbers."

"Right again."

"Well," Hunter said, "since I don't intend to have anyone smuggle money out of town, I don't think I have anything to worry about."

"I'm just letting you know," Clint said, "I'll be watching."

"And I will, too," the mayor said, "watching you go right out that door."

"Just remember," Clint said, and left.

***

Clint had no intention of watching the street. What he was going to do was watch the mayor's house. The only place the mayor could wait for Duffy to approach with the money without being seen was inside his house. And the only time to do that was at night, in the dark.

But just to be on the safe side, Clint found himself a doorway directly across the street from City Hall. That's where he was when Edward Lowry returned from his meeting with Mike Duffy—a meeting Clint Adams didn't know for sure had taken place, but was hoping for.

***

When Lowry entered, the mayor Hunter said, "Shut the damned door!"

Lowry closed it and sat.

"Well?"

"Duffy will stay away from the Gunsmith today," Lowry said. "Tonight, he'll bring the money to your house."

"Good," Hunter said. "Clint Adams was just here, and he's going to be watching for anybody leaving town with the money."

"How would he know?" Lowry asked.

"Money from three banks?" the mayor asked, his eyes shining with greed. "That's got to be a big load."

"As a matter of fact," Lowry said, "Duffy had a duffle bag at his feet in the Red Rose."

"Jesus, out in the open?" Hunter said, then laughed. "The man's got balls, I'll say that for him."

"He was keeping it right where he could protect it, I guess," Lowry said.

"All right, as long as he stays out of sight until tonight we should be okay," Hunter said.

"When do I get paid?" Lowry asked.

"Don't worry, Edward," Hunter said. "I haven't forgotten your part in all this. As soon as I get the money from Duffy, we'll start on the next phase of my plan. But you'll get your end of this job before that."

Lowry said, "Okay," although what he was thinking was, I better.

***

Duffy had dug up the money and stuffed it into the bag early that morning. Now he had to figure out what to do with it until dark.

He wondered if he should just walk down Main Street with the bag and let the Gunsmith challenge him, and get that part of the job over with, despite what the mayor said. But in the end, he thought, no, he had better do what the politician said if he wanted to move on with the man to bigger, better and richer jobs.

He waved to the bartender and when the man came over he said, "Steve, I need your back room."

Since Steve Hudson was afraid of Mike Duffy he said, "Sure, Mike, whatever you need."

***

When neither Lowry nor the mayor came back out, Clint started to feel more positive about his plan. Hopefully, this would all come to an end that night, with the mayor and his bank robbing cronies together in the dark at the mayor's house.

Where else would Mayor Hunter feel safe receiving the spoils of his plan to rob his own town? Clint had to give the man credit. Most politicians did their stealing on a much smaller scale. Hubert Hunter was thinking on a much larger scale.

Chapter Forty-Six

Mayor Hubert Hunter poured himself a brandy and wondered if he was making a mistake. Not in planning the bank robberies to coincide with the Miss Dance Hall contest, but in having Mike Duffy bring the money there to his house? But where else would have made sense? Hunter didn't see himself meeting Duffy in some dark, dank, dismal back street saloon.

Lowry wanted to be there, but Hunter said no. Lowry didn't know he was on his way out. That was going to be another job for Mike Duffy. But first, the money exchange.

He sat down in his most comfortable chair and waited.

***

Clint was across the street from the mayor's house, not in a doorway, but in some bushes. He was taking the chance that Duffy would be so confident that the man would simply go in the front door. If he went in the back way, this might not turn out the way Clint wanted it to. But he didn't have anyone to back his play. He couldn't depend on the sheriff, and he didn't want to use the sheriff's young deputies. There was nobody else to press into service.

So he squatted, and waited.

***

Mike Duffy grabbed the bag of money from the back room of the Red Rose Saloon, hiked it up onto his shoulder, and went out the back door into the dark. He headed for the mayor's house. When he got there, he went in through the back door, which Hunter had left unlocked.

If that was all there was to it, Clint would have been beat.

***

Edward Lowry checked his watch, saw that the time was right. He opened the top drawer of his desk, took out a gun and tucked it into his belt, then stood up and left City Hall.

***

Clint recognize the man approaching the mayor's house as Lowry. He wasn't carrying any kind of bag, but as he got to the front door he took a gun from his belt.

There was a hijack in progress.

***

Clint stood and broke from his cover, assuming everyone involved was now inside.

***

Mike Duffy had just put the bag of money down on the coffee table in front of the mayor when there was a knock at the front door.

"You expecting anybody else?" he asked Hunter.

"No."

"Adams?" Duffy asked.

"Would he knock?" Hunter said. "Maybe Lowry. Something might be up. You wait here."

Mayor Hunter went to the door.

***

As Hunter appeared in the doorway Lowry pointed his gun at the man's face.

"Not a word."

"Wha—"

"Shh! Duffy inside? Just nod or shake your head."

Hunter nodded.

199

"Back up."

He did, and Lowry entered.

***

Clint was on the run across the street. He waited for a shot, but apparently Lowry wasn't ready to kill the mayor. They stepped into the house and the front door closed. He only hoped it hadn't locked.

***

Lowry backed the mayor into the house, and the living room.

"Who was it—" Duffy started turning. When he saw Lowry and the gun, he tensed.

"Don't, Duffy!" Lowry snapped, pointing the gun at him. "I don't think you're that fast."

Duffy thought about it, then moved his hand away from his gun.

"Use your left hand and drop it."

Duffy did so, reaching across his body, plucking his gun from his holster, and dropping it to the floor. Lowry's eyes were on the bag on the coffee table. He had seen it before, in the Red Rose, sitting at Duffy's feet.

"What are you trying to pull, Lowry?" the mayor asked.

"Just making sure I get my share, Mr. Mayor," he said, "and more."

"There is more," Hunter said. "Plenty more, in Fort Worth. Now we know the plan works."

"If you want to wait to rob some Fort Worth banks during the Miss Texas contest, that's up to you. I'm going to take mine now. If you don't mind."

"I mind," Clint said.

***

Clint found the front door open and slipped into the house. He could hear voice from inside and followed them. He saw the man he assumed was Mike Duffy take his gun from his holster with his left hand and drop it at his feet. Lowry was foolish enough not to tell the man to kick it away.

He listened, heard what the mayor's plan was for Fort Worth, and decided to make his move.

" . . . if you don't mind," Lowry said.

Clint stepped out and said, "I mind."

He hadn't expected the smaller man to move so quickly, so he had no choice. As Lowry turned on him with his gun already in his hand, Clint drew and fired. The bullet struck Lowry in the chest, drove him back until he landed right on the bag of money.

The coffee table then collapsed beneath his weight.

Duffy didn't waste any time. He bent to retrieve his gun, started to bring it to bear on Clint, who fired again. Duffy was still moving, the bullet struck him in the belly. His mouth gaped open, his gun fell from his now paralyzed hand. He slumped forward and fell atop Lowry, who was still lying on the money bag.

"There's a lot of money in that bag, Adams," Mayor Hunter said. "Fifty-fifty?" His tone was hopeful.

Clint just looked at the man and shook his head.

Chapter Forty-Seven

Clint woke two mornings later, in Rita's bed. She was lying next to him, on her back, the bedsheet down around her waist so that her marvelous breasts were in view. He leaned over, tongued first one nipple, then the other, then repeated the action until she moaned and stretched her arms up over her head.

"What a nice way to wake up," she said, then opened her eyes wide and looked at him. "But . . . you're leaving today."

"I am."

"Then this is good-bye?"

"All last night was good-bye."

"Oh no," she said, dropping her arms so they were around his neck. "I want a morning goodbye."

"Never let it be said I left a beautiful woman wanting," he said, and bent to the task . . .

***

Later she watched him dress.

"So will you be going to Fort Worth for the big contest?" he asked.

"Oh, no," she said, "I have no interest. Will you?"

"No, I'm finished with beauty contests, and that in-cludes Fort Worth. But . . . it's a shame Hermione won't have someone with her."

"But she will," Rita said. "Both Penny and Amy will be going with her."

"It's nice of them to support her."

"Well, it's not entirely to support her," Rita said. "Af-ter all, Amy came in second. If Hermione should sprain an ankle, or something . . ."

"Then I guess Hermione better watch her step, huh?"

"And her back," Rita said.

"Oh, you don't think the sisters would . . ."

"You never know," she said. "Now, come kiss me goodbye and then go quickly . . ."

***

He collected Eclipse from the livery stable, then rode down Main Street, stopping to talk to Randall Flatt who was sweeping the boardwalk in front of his store.

"Well, this is a comedown from running the contest, isn't it?" he asked.

"I don't have a choice," he said, leaning on the broom, "Adele has me on K-P duty to make up for the time I spent away from the store. Although . . ."

"Yes?"

" . . . she does seem to be in a better frame of mind, lately. It's as if something happened to lighten her spirit." Flatt frowned. "I wonder what that could be?"

Clint had an idea, but he said, "Maybe she's just glad to have her husband back . . . oh, and your money back in the bank."

"I think the whole town's happy about that," Flatt said. "After giving the money back I bet you could stay here and run for mayor."

"Oh, not me," Clint said. "The last thing I want to be is a politician. But what about you? I bet you could win. After all, we took the money back to the banks together."

"Now that's a thought," Flatt said. "If I won I'd probably have to give up the store, but then Adele would be the first lady around here. I bet that would make her happy."

"I bet some attention from her husband would do that," Clint said.

Flatt didn't seem to hear him. He was deep in thought about possibly becoming mayor.

"Well," Clint said, "good luck with whatever you decide, Randall."

"Huh? Oh, yeah, thanks for everything, Clint."

"Yes," Adele said, coming out the door behind her husband, "thank you for *everything,* Mr. Adams."

Clint got out of Redwind as fast as Eclipse could carry him.

Coming February 27, 2019

THE GUNSMITH
444
Deadly Trouble

For more information
visit: www.SpeakingVolumes.us

Coming Spring 2019

Lady Gunsmith 7
Roxy Doyle and the James Boys

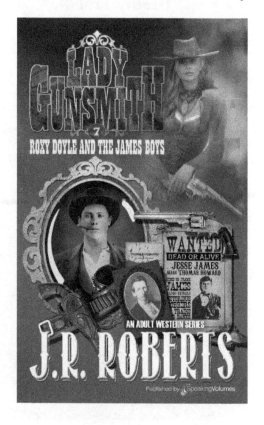

For more information
visit:

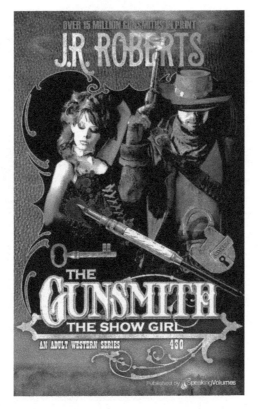

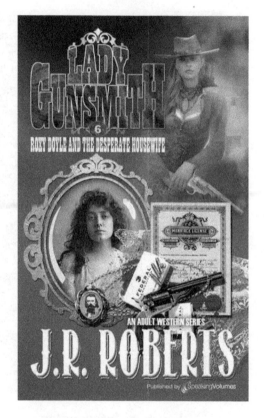

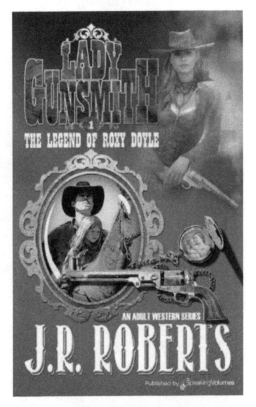

On Sale Now!

MOUNTAIN JACK PIKE *series*
by
Award-Winning Author
Robert J. Randisi (J.R. Roberts)

For more information
visit: www.speakingvolumes.us

50% Off
Audiobooks

As Low As $5.00 Each
While Supplies Last!

Free Shipping
(to the 48 contiguous United States)

For more information
visit: www.HalfPriceAudiobooks.com

Sign up for free and bargain books

Join the Speaking Volumes mailing list

Text

ILOVEBOOKS

to 22828 to get started.